PCH

Taken

A PORT CITY HIGH NOVEL

SHANNON FREEMAN

SADDLEBACK
EDUCATIONAL PUBLISHING

High School High

Taken

Deported

The Public Eye

The Accident

Listed

Traumatized

A Port in Pieces

www.sdlback.com

Copyright ©2013 by Saddleback Educational Publishing

ISBN-13: 978-1-62250-038-3
ISBN-10: 1-62250-038-5
eBook: 978-1-61247-681-0

Printed in Guangzhou, China
NOR/0715/CA21501090

19 18 17 16 15   2 3 4 5 6

ACKNOWLEDGMENTS

First I have to first say thank you to the Creator for entrusting me with the gift of writing. I just pray that I am a good vessel for the messages that he has placed on my heart.

Thanks to my husband, Derrick Freeman. You are my everything. You are truly God given. Thank you, thank you, thank you for giving me the family I've always wanted and the love I've always needed. The day we cleaved together is when my life truly began.

Thanks to my mother, Carolyn Warrick. I will probably thank you in every book I write. You are my rock.

Thanks to my father, Glenn Ford, for inspiring me.

Thanks to my sister, Rochelle Jenkins. You are the person who just gets me, and I'm so blessed because of our relationship. If I could have chosen the perfect parts to create my own sister, those parts would still make you. Thank you for always being there for me.

I don't know many people who can say that they've had the same friends since fourth grade, but I can. Felisha Francis Collins and Shannon Woods Richard, I couldn't let another book go by without telling you how truly blessed I am for having you in my life. It's as if God knew that we would need each other. You are both priceless.

—Shannon Freeman

DEDICATION

This book is dedicated to all the students whom I have had the privilege to teach. If you can see it, you can be it. I love each and every one of you, and I'm somewhere rooting for your success.

Prologue

*L*ife was just getting back to normal for Brandi, Shane, and Marisa. The long Christmas break was over, and memories were all that remained. What a crazy time! Shane kicked her drug habit again, and Brandi and Marisa mended their friendship that was almost torn apart by Brandi's first love, Matthew.

Before the break, their first semester of high school had not been what they had imagined. Today, as they loaded up in Shane's mom's Tahoe, they were just thankful that they were all still friends.

"Ouch!" Shane said as Brandi jumped into the car. "You looking all Christmas-present cute today," she said, laughing.

"Stop clowning. You know I bought this jacket when we went shopping. At least during the winter, our coats and scarves can add a little swag to these boring uniforms."

"I hate uniforms, especially when it's cold. I can't even wear my Uggs. They trippin'," Shane replied.

"Um, ladies, stop complaining. It's your first day back at school. You both should be thankful that we are all sitting here. This wasn't an easy winter break for any of us," Mrs. Foster said as she pulled up in front of Marisa's house. Mrs. Foster had suffered as much as any of them. Shane's little drug experiment and her older sister's pregnancy announcement had been a bit much for the Fosters.

"You're right, Mom," Shane replied.

"Did I hear your correctly, Shane? Did you say I was right?"

"There's a first time for everything, Mrs. Foster," Brandi teased.

"Shush," Shane said, reaching over and slugging her in the arm.

"Hey, hey, hey," Marisa said as she got into the truck. "Y'all too cool for school. Hey, Mrs. Foster! Thanks for picking me up."

"Did you just get that? It's adorable," Shane said, admiring Marisa's powder blue jacket.

"Mama gave it to me last night. It was love at first sight. Hey, I'm a poet!"

"You're also a geek, but we love you anyway." Brandi laughed as she gave Shane a high five.

"Don't be j," Marisa said as she laughed along with her friends. "Jealousy doesn't become you."

Mrs. Foster pulled up in front of Port City High. "Well, ladies, enjoy yourselves today. Remember, high school is the best time of your life."

"Mom, you have to stop saying that. Surely life will get better than this," Shane said dryly. It was hard for her to believe that these were her best days. She had so much more planned for herself.

"Just keep saying good morning, Shane. Just keep saying good morning."

"Bye, Mom," Shane said, rolling her eyes. It was probably the thousandth time that she had heard that phrase. A quick exit was necessary when Mrs. Foster started dropping nuggets of wisdom on them.

The girls jumped out of the truck and were greeted by cold winter air that contrasted sharply with the warmth from the heater.

As they walked into the school, they were ushered into the auditorium for a welcome-back program.

CHAPTER 1

Marisa

Crowded hallways, clanging lockers, and students running in all directions, it was the background music of high school. Marisa soaked it all in as she hurried from class to class. She settled into her science class, and her teacher began to address the requirements for this half of the school year. Marisa's mind wandered off to the first semester. She thought about Brandi's middle school boyfriend, Matthew Kincade. She and Brandi had almost ruined their friendship over him. The ironic part was that after all the dust had settled, Brandi had given her approval for Marisa and Matthew to date, but he had already moved on to some other girl.

Marisa was a bit relieved. When she fell in love, she wanted it to be with someone whom her friends could be comfortable around. A relationship with Matthew would have been anything but comfortable.

She thought back to how it started, so simple, so innocent. They were just two friends who were thrust into six of their seven classes together. It's no wonder they were feeling closer than normal, especially with his parents looming divorce and her beef with her arch nemesis, Ashley. As she looked around the room, she noticed that Matthew wasn't there. He hadn't been in any of her classes so far; however, she had seen him in the hall that morning. *He must have gone home sick*, she thought.

Marisa's last class was Theatre Arts. She learned that the school play was in April, and tryouts were in two weeks. She had been in drama in middle school and had always excelled. But now she was in the big pond. She had never had small parts before. She wondered which play it would be. No matter what, she was going to work hard. She was determined to have the part she wanted memorized in time for tryouts.

When drama class was over, she looked for Shane in the crowded hallway. Since school was letting out it was nearly impossible to find anyone. Second semester was always so different. There was no more twirling practice to run to. She was a regular girl now, not one who would be on the field Friday night in front of the hundreds of football fans.

This play was just what she needed. It would take the place of twirling. Her mama always told her, "*Mi hija*, an idle mind is the devil's playground." It was one of the reasons she stayed as busy as possible: school work, extracurricular activities. Plus she still found time to study the modeling world. Marisa had exotic beauty that came from her Hispanic background, and she was getting taller every day. People always told her that she would be a great model. She wanted to prove them right.

Just as she was being pushed through the hallway by the natural flow of students attempting to make a quick exit from school, she ran into Matthew and a cute little freshman that she had seen around school. *Not another one*, she thought.

"Hey, Matt," Marisa said nervously. She was uncomfortable, but for some strange reason, she felt nothing for this guy that she was willing to risk her friendship with Brandi over only a month before.

"Hey, Mari! How was your first day back?"

"It was straight. I thought that you went home today. I didn't see you in any of our classes."

"Oh yeah ... the counselor called me

out of homeroom and gave me a new schedule. I don't have any of the same classes anymore," he said while trying to avoid eye contact.

"Oh, that's strange," she said, noticing how uncomfortable he was. The girl on Matt's arm cleared her throat and gave him a nudge, breaking up their conversation.

"Oh, my bad," Matthew said. "This is Lauren."

"Nice to meet you," Lauren said as she looked Marisa up and down, slowly sizing up her former competition.

Marisa felt sideswiped. Did this girl know about her and Matt? Surely he hadn't confided in her. "Nice to meet you too," Marisa said, looking her directly in the eyes, letting her know that she didn't shake her.

Matthew could obviously feel the tension and decided it was time to make a quick exit. "All right, stay up, Mari. We have to get going."

"Okay, Matt. *So* nice to meet you, Lauren," Marisa said with a hint of sarcasm.

"Yeah, you too, Marisa," Lauren said with a sly grin, slipping her arm inside Matt's.

This broad was really feeling herself. Marisa never liked girls like her. Marisa was prettier than most girls in her class, but somehow she stayed humble. This girl was just the opposite. She was a true jump-off groupie that Matthew had decided was worth being on his arm. "Good luck with that one, Mattie," Marisa whispered as she turned away from them and continued her hunt for Shane.

CHAPTER 2

Shane

Shane searched the crowded hallway for either Marisa or Brandi. She checked her phone. School had let out five minutes before. What could be taking them so long? She was ready to head over to Jerry's, their favorite burger spot. It would be packed on the first day back at school. It was probably the last day that they wouldn't be inundated with after-school activities and homework.

She felt somebody pinch her leg and swung around, but nobody was there. When she turned back toward the locker, she saw Brandi giggling. "Quit playing," she said as if she was mad, but they both knew that she was only pretending.

She could see Marisa's head bobbing through the hallway in a crowd of students. She was coming their way with a huge smile on her face. "Good thing you're tall. I can spot you in any crowd," she said as Marisa walked up.

"I am *so* ready to eat!" Marisa declared.

"Me too," Brandi said, looking up from her locker. "Call Robin and see if she wants me to swoop the car for her."

"Brandi, you can't even drive. Why would she want you to do that?" Shane asked.

"Just trying to help. You know pregnant people can't walk far, but if you feel that way about it, then, hey, I won't drive. Call and check Robie's coordinates, and we can meet her out front."

"Knowing preggo pop, she's already out there waiting. There *is* food involved."

"True," the girls said in unison as they headed outside. Just as they thought, they spotted Robin's car from the steps and immediately started laughing.

"What took y'all so long? I've been waiting here forever."

"We're not that late. What's your problem?" Shane asked.

"I don't have to drive y'all around. How many other girls do you see out here picking up their sister and her friends? None!" Robin exclaimed.

Brandi's eyebrows immediately went up. "Her sister's friends? So we ain't cool or something?" she asked.

"Robie, you tripping. We just went to our lockers and came out," Marisa chimed in.

"Look, ladies, I can't do this right now. I won't be your ride this semester. I'm cutting y'all off. I have my own issues I need to tend to."

The girls' mouths dropped open. For a moment there was complete silence in the car. "Well, we cutting you off too, then. How 'bout that?" Shane spat.

"What do you mean, 'you're cutting *me* off'?"

"Just what I said. Your three baby-sitters quit—in advance. Nah!"

"For the past two years, I have been the one person you could call on at anytime to go anywhere, and you're cutting me off because I need a break?"

Shane was livid. Robin was being impossible. Seriously? What was the big deal?

Robin pulled up at Jerry's. The girls jumped out. They watched Robin peel out of the parking lot. "Well, I guess we need to find a ride home, ladies," Shane declared as they went inside.

CHAPTER 3

Brandi

After eating some snacks and catching up, Brandi said, "I'll call and see if my mom is getting off anytime s—Hey! My purse is gone. I'm going to check in the restroom." She searched frantically in the restroom, then returned to the table empty handed. "Are you sure you don't have my bag?" she asked her friends.

"No, and we asked the manager if anyone had turned it in. No luck," Shane said. "Hey, my mom's outside. What do you want to do?"

"I have to get home. I don't know how somebody could have taken my purse without me noticing. Nothing like this ever happens here. I'm going to talk to the manager myself. I'll meet you at the car."

Brandi asked the manager about the security cameras, but they weren't working. She was simply out of luck: no money, no house keys, and no Coach bag. What a day!

"What did they say?" Mrs. Foster asked Brandi when she got to the truck.

"Nothing really, they'll keep an eye out for it," Brandi said, sounding defeated.

"Well, I'm sure it'll turn up," Mrs. Foster said.

As soon as Brandi walked through the door, Mrs. Haywood said, "Where have you been? Raven wanted to tell you all about school, and you—"

"How was your day, Brandi? Oh, it was horrible, Mom, and yours?" Brandi mumbled under her breath. She'd had enough drama dealing with Robin and having her purse stolen. She didn't need her mom jumping all over her too.

That stopped Mrs. Haywood in her tracks. "What happened now?"

"I think somebody stole my purse when I was at Jerry's. We looked everywhere, but it just vanished."

"That is horrible, baby. I'm so sorry. I just hate that your ID and keys are in there. That always scares me. Guess I'll be changing the locks."

"I'm sure nobody would break in, Mom. They probably just wanted money."

"Never can be too careful. I'll call them to come out tomorrow."

Raven came running down the stairs. "Hey, Brandi," she said, giving her a huge hug.

"Hey, li'l mama! How was your day?" she asked, kissing Raven on the forehead.

"It was all right. Mom's cooking dinner tonight! Lasagna!" she said, doing the latest dance move. "When's the food going to be ready, Mom? What time are we eating?"

"Well, I keep trying to call your father, but he's not answering. Did you talk to him today?" her mother asked.

"No, but I can give him a call." Brandi used the house phone and left her dad a message. She hated when he didn't answer his phone. "No answer, Mom. Call me when y'all are ready to eat. I'm going upstairs." Once her homework was completed, Brandi decided she was too hungry to wait on anybody to call her for dinner. She was in the mood to eat and get in the shower. *What is taking Dad so long anyway*, she wondered.

When she went back downstairs, she could hear her mother whispering into the phone, "Now this is just not cool. The girls have been waiting for you. It's their first day back at school. Call me as soon as you get this. I'm getting sick of this."

"Mom, are you okay?"

Brandi's mother spun around quickly with tears in her eyes. "Yes, baby. Let's go ahead and start eating. Will you help me set the table?"

"Sure," Brandi said, eyeing her mother. "Mom, why don't you go upstairs and wash up? I can handle the table on my own."

Her mother nodded and left the room. After Brandi finished setting the table, she headed upstairs to get Raven. She was watching TV and laughing without a care in the world. "Hey, baby girl. We're about to eat."

"Did Dad make it home?" she asked excitedly.

"Nah, he's going to be later than we expected. We'll have to start without him."

When they sat down to eat, Brandi noticed her mother just moving food around her plate. She was there with them, but it seemed that her mind was somewhere else. Her laughter was empty, and Brandi could see she was battling to hold back tears.

"Hey, squirt, head upstairs and take your bath. I'll get the kitchen cleaned up," Brandi told Raven.

"But, B, it's my night to clean up."

"I know, but I want to. Now scoot."

Mrs. Haywood and Brandi cleared the dishes from the table. "You know he's okay, right?" she asked her mom.

"Huh? Oh yeah, baby ... I know."

"This isn't the first time he's disappeared. He always comes back."

Her mother looked at her for a minute. "You're getting older, Brandi, but it's still my job to protect you. You should be worried about school and having fun, not about drama at home."

"Look, Mom. Sometimes we have drama at home. It's not your fault. I know I don't always act like I get it, but I know who my father is. I know what he is. He's an addict who puts drugs before his family. It ain't that hard," she said with an attitude.

"Don't go there, Brandi," her mother said in a stern voice. "Just leave it alone." Brandi could sense that her mom was hanging on by a thread. She knew it was time to back off. Her mom never wanted to talk about her dad's dangerous habit. They continued to clean in silence. There was nothing left to say.

When they were done with the dishes, Brandi kissed her mom and headed upstairs to shower and get her clothes ready for school the next day. After she wrapped her hair, she lay down in bed to watch TV. Before she knew it, she was asleep.

CHAPTER 4

Coming Home

"All I know is that I don't ever want to get pregnant," Marisa said as the girls video chatted.

"I know. Me neither," Shane responded. "My sister has always been feisty, but she has taken it to a whole other level with this pregnancy. I know she's under a lot of pressure, but it's getting harder and harder to bite my tongue. I hope this baby just hurries up outta there."

"Leave that baby where it is," Marisa said. "It's not done baking yet."

"I know. I'm just glad that the health of

your baby is not determined by how mean you are."

"Girl, stop," Brandi chimed in, laughing. "Give her some time. I remember how snappy my mom was when she was pregnant with Raven. It will pass, and we will have our Robin back."

"Yeah, till the postpartum kicks in ... lucky me!"

"Well, baby girl, this time it's not about you. It's about Robin, so get over yourself," Marisa said, trying to snap her back to reality.

"Okay ... enough about me. Anything new with you two?"

"Nothing here, except getting ready for the play. I have tryouts in less than a week now. I want to have all the lines memorized for at least two roles. I really don't want to wind up as an extra," Marisa said.

"I'm sure you'll do fine. You always do," Shane encouraged. "What about you, B?"

"Nothing here ... same ole same,"

Brandi lied. They hadn't seen her father in days. Her mother was crying all the time, and she was trying to put on a brave face for Raven. She never shared her family's business. She was much too private. "I'm just glad it's basketball season. I love cheering indoors. Outside is so humid."

"Uh-oh," Shane said.

"Uh-huh," Marisa said.

"What?" Brandi asked.

"Girl, every time you start talking about the weather, it means that something is wrong, and you are trying to avoid talking about it," Shane said, calling her out.

Brandi rolled her eyes. "Look—"

Just as she was about to tell them to back off, Raven burst through her door. "Brandi, he's home; Dad's back."

"I gotta go."

"Wait, Brandi, what's going on over there?" Marisa asked, concerned. But Brandi was gone.

"What was that about?" Shane asked.

"I have no idea."

"She didn't say anything to you?"

"Not a thing. Raven sounded really upset, though," Marisa said.

"Why would she be upset that Mr. Haywood was home? That's crazy," Shane responded.

"Do you think we should do something?"

"What can we do? Sounds like it's family stuff. The best thing we can do is be there for her if she asks. We can't get all in their business."

"True. Well, I'll see you in the morning. I need to finish up on this algebra homework," Marisa announced.

"Cool, I'll hit you on Friender later."

"Girl, I'm in Friender rehab. I can't spend my whole life on a social network."

"Whatever ... just log on later so we can chat."

"If I get through with my homework, it's a deal!"

CHAPTER 5

Brandi

Brandi and Raven watched in shock as their father rocked in their mother's arms on the living room floor. It had been three days since they had seen him. He was wearing the same clothes, and they could smell a stench coming from him all the way up the stairs. Normally Brandi would have protected Raven from the disturbing scene, but she was in shock too. Where had he been? What had happened to him?

It seemed like forever that they sat there. Tears poured down each of their faces. Her father cried for what he had been through and the pain that he caused his family; her mother cried with relief. When her mother saw the girls, she froze. Never would she have wanted them to see their father in this state. She locked eyes with Brandi, who knew what her mother wanted. She wanted the girls to leave and let them deal with this as husband and wife.

Brandi led her sister upstairs. "Brandi, can I sleep in your room tonight?" Raven asked.

"Sure, baby girl. Just go get some extra pillows from your room." It had been a long week. They both needed each other.

Brandi got some snacks out for them and turned on *Dreamgirls*, their favorite movie. "Brandi, what happened to Dad?"

Brandi had to bite back a snappy remark about her father. "He's just sick. That's all. Don't you worry about a thing. Let's just watch our movie."

She knew that her parents would need some privacy, so she turned the volume up a couple of notches on the TV. They cuddled up close to each other and fell asleep, just like when Raven was a toddler.

The next morning when Brandi woke up, the night before felt like a bad dream. Her head was hurting; she had tossed and turned all night. Raven had cried several times during the night.

When she arrived downstairs, breakfast was already on the table. Her mother had worked hard to make life look normal, but her father was nowhere in sight. "Where's Dad?" Brandi asked dryly.

"Honey, your father is lying down. He's not feeling well right now."

"I bet!"

"Brandi, not today, baby. Mama's dealing with enough."

Just then Raven came running down the stairs. "Where's Dad?"

"Your father is lying down, my baby. You'll see him this afternoon when you get home," she said, kissing Raven's forehead as she handed her a plate of bacon, eggs, and toast.

"I want cereal."

Mrs. Haywood looked as though she were about to lose it. "Raven—"

Brandi cut her off. "Raven, just eat what Mom cooked. It looks like she worked hard on breakfast today."

Mrs. Haywood gave Brandi a "Thank you" with her eyes and went to get herself together for work.

Brandi ate her breakfast, took two aspirin, made sure Raven got on her bus, and headed out the door for school.

As soon as she sat down in class, she realized that she hadn't done any of her homework. With a night like she had, she could not have cared less. When Mrs. Sumner came around to check everybody's homework, Brandi had none.

"Where is your research homework, Brandi?" Mrs. Sumner asked when she walked by Brandi's desk.

"I forgot about it."

"Well then, you have to stay after school so that you can catch up to the rest of the class. You have to have the research complete to move on to the next phase of the scientific method."

Brandi looked at Mrs. Sumner as if she had just exited the crazy train. "That ain't happening. I have cheerleader practice after school and a game tomorrow night."

Mrs. Sumner was taken aback. Brandi had never spoken to her this way. "Excuse me, Brandi?"

"I said that ain't happening."

"You watch your tone with me, young lady, before you get sent out of here."

"I could not care less if you send me out," she spat at Mrs. Sumner. "I'll do you one better, I'll just leave." And with that, Brandi was out the door. You could have heard a pin drop in the classroom as Brandi's exit stunned her classmates. Brandi went straight to the office. When her referral arrived, she was called into the principal's office. The principal got on the phone with Mrs. Haywood. *Whatever,* she thought. *She needs to go tend to her husband and stay outta my business.*

Brandi's whole demeanor was different. The week had taken a toll on her. She sat slouched in her chair with a scowl on her face as Mrs. Montgomery finished talking to her mom, "I see ... I will ... thank you, Mrs. Haywood."

"Brandi, your mother told me that you had a pretty rough night." Brandi didn't respond. "Do you want to talk about it?"

"No."

"Well, Brandi, even though you are having problems at home, you can't come here and take it out on everyone else—"

"Okay. Can I go?" Brandi said, cutting her principal off.

"Brandi, I've never seen this side of you before. Are you sure you don't want to talk about this? Your mother wasn't specific, but if it's something that I could help you with, I'll do my best."

Brandi laughed. "No, Mrs. Montgomery. It's nothing that you can help me with." Who can help you when your father chooses drugs over his family? Who can help you when your little sister is growing up in chaos? Who can help you when you are basically raising yourself and nobody's there for you because they are always dealing with addiction? Nobody! Nobody can help you with that.

CHAPTER 6

Marisa

The newness of the year was wearing off, and everyone was business as usual. For Marisa, life was just about to get hectic. Auditions for the school play were today. When she picked up the script last week, she was thrilled that they would be doing *The Wizard of Oz*. She was a huge fan. She really wanted to play Dorothy. But there was no way the lead role would go to a ninth grader. Even though she knew it was a long shot, she memorized the part. She was also trying out for the part of the Wicked Witch. Her main goal was to avoid the usual ninth-grader fate: an extra or an understudy.

Before Marisa knew it, she was sitting in the auditorium with all of the other aspiring actors. She nervously looked over her script.

She was trying to get mentally prepared when she felt someone plop in the seat next to her. *All the seats in this auditorium and this fool has to come and sit right next to me.* Then she felt a nudge. She was just about to snap when she looked over to see Shane smiling at her. "What are you doing here?" she asked, confused.

"Trying out for the school play, hello," Shane told her.

"Why didn't you tell me? I had no idea," Marisa said excitely.

"Oh, what fun would that have been? You have your lines memorized?"

"Yeah, I memorized Dorothy and the Wicked Witch."

"Oh, my girl got it like that, huh? A

freshman trying out for the lead? I love it."

"Whoa, not so much pressure, Shane, k? I'm already nervous enough. What part are you trying out for?"

"The Good Witch! I love the costume. I want to be in all white. You know how good I look in white," Shane said happily.

"Shane, I'm not trying to be a Debbie Downer, but are you up for all of this? This play is going to be a lot of work. You are already on the school newspaper; yearbook is coming up. I'm concerned that you are going to overload yourself again."

Last semester had been a nightmare for Shane. She felt so overwhelmed that she started taking Adderall to give her more energy. Her only focus now was her schoolwork and the school newspaper. But she was going to add the school play to her schedule.

"Don't worry about me, Mari. Seriously, I need to stay busy. Robin is driving me crazy. She's so moody and irritable."

"I feel you, but just promise me that if the pressure gets to be too much, you'll talk to me or Brandi about it instead of taking drastic measures."

"That's a promise! I definitely will."

"Marisa Maldonado, Hayley Brooks, Hannah Cooper, and Ashley Rivera will be reading for the part of Dorothy. Can you girls make your way to the stage please?"

"Oh my God! Did you hear that list? The feature twirler, star of last year's play, my archenemy, and me ... great ... I'm not nervous at all," Marisa whispered to Shane as she headed to the stage. Her legs felt like spaghetti.

"You'll be fine," Shane said, laughing.

Watching this group of girls go at it was like watching the final episode of *Top Model*. It was great. Shane had to admit, there was a lot of talent on that stage, but Mari was holding her own.

When Mari returned to her seat, she was a new person. She was in her zone and any nervousness she had before was gone when she hit the stage. She was in her element, and it showed.

"Wow, Mari! You did great."

"Please, they did great. I had to blow it out of the park to take the lead from a senior. Hey, they're calling you. Break a leg."

When Shane walked onstage, she looked like the Good Witch. She had chosen to wear all white to school that day, even though it was still winter. With her white down jacket and her white jeans that hugged every curve, it wasn't a stretch that she at least looked the part.

After her audition, she was beaming. "That was so fun. I love theater!" she said, excited as she returned to her seat.

Mari was next; she still had not read for the Wicked Witch. She wasn't nervous anymore, and the other girls trying out for this role didn't intimidate her so much. When she finished her audition, the crowd erupted. She was phenomenal. "That was awesome, Mari."

"Thanks! It felt right. Now let's go to Jerry's. I'm starving."

"We don't have ride. How are we supposed to get there?"

"We can ride with Hayley. She just sent me a text seeing if we wanted to roll with them."

"Really? Hayley has never been my cup of tea," Shane said, a little skeptical about rolling with Marisa's other crew.

"Aw, don't be so hard on her. She's a lot like us. You just have to get to know her."

"Maybe she's a lot like you, but she's nothing like me."

"Shane, be a good sport."

"Okay, but if you see me pulling my hair out, then you know it's time to bounce," she said, half playing and half serious.

CHAPTER 7

Shane

Dinner with Hayley had been exactly how Shane pictured it. Hayley was always used to being front and center, and it carried over into her personal life. She didn't seem to know how to keep it on the field.

"Well, I gotta get home," Shane announced. "Are y'all about ready?"

"Sure," Hayley said. Using her handheld mirror, she touched up her lip gloss and smoothed any wayward strands of hair. She swung the latest Juicy Couture handbag over her shoulder and was ready to ride. "I'll take you ladies home."

When Shane got home, she went straight to Robin's room to tell her about auditions and talk about how ridiculous she thought Hayley was.

"Robie, open the door," she said. Shane missed her sister so much. Sometimes she wished they could be just like they used to be.

"Hey, Shane. How was your day?"

"It was pretty awesome. I tried out for the school play. What'd you do?"

"Girl, more of the same ole same. Hey, I wanted to apologize for leaving y'all at Jerry's the other day. This pregnancy thing has me all over the place."

"Yeah, I noticed. I just had dinner with Marisa and Hayley. Do you know her?"

"Yeah, I know Hayley. We've been in school together forever. She is in my class, ya know?"

"Yeah, I know. She just doesn't seem like the type of girl you kick it with."

"And she's not. When was the last time

she came over here? Exactly. Never."

"She's so—"

"Superficial," Robin completed the sentence for her.

"Well, if I knew what that meant ... probably," Shane said, laughing

"Shallow, Shane, it means shallow. You need to read more. You're a writer now for Pete's sake," her sister joked.

"So how have you been? Are you and Gavin okay? How is he handling all of this?"

"He's handling it. We are about to be parents, Shane. That's crazy." Tears started to form in her eyes.

"What's wrong, Robie?

"I'm too young to be a mother. What do I know about life? I've been sitting here trying to figure out what to teach this child. I don't want to mess this little person up. It's just a lot, ya know?"

Shane had never seen Robin so unsure of herself. She was a very confident girl, but today was different. She sat right next to her sister and put her arms around her. "You are going to be an excellent mother. Look at how much practice you had raising me."

Robin began to cry even harder. "And look how you turned out," she sobbed. Both girls lost it and began laughing uncontrollably. It made them both feel so much better when they had each other.

CHAPTER 8

Friender Fever

Shane and Marisa searched frantically for their names on the wall near the Theatre Arts room. "You see my name?" Shane asked.

"I'm looking, I'm looking," Marisa replied as she towered over the other students who were looking for their own names on the list. Everyone was anxious. "I'm not Dorothy," she whispered to Shane, who was close by and trying to maneuver to the front of the crowd.

Finally Shane pushed through to the front and the first name that she saw was her own. She had gotten the part of the Good Witch, and right underneath was Marisa's name for the part of the Wicked Witch. Shane saw her name at the same time Marisa saw hers, and they began to celebrate together.

Brandi was close by, engrossed in her phone. "How'd it go?" she asked.

"You are laying your eyes on the Good Witch," Shane said, adding in an innocent curtsy.

"And the Wicked Witch," Marisa said as she took her first bow.

"Two witches? How fitting!" Brandi said mischievously.

"Hush," Shane said, giving her a hip bump. "Let's go celebrate! Jerry's. On me!"

"I'm down. Let's roll out."

Just as they were about to part, they saw Ashley pushing her way through the crowd to search for her name on the list. She read through the names once. Then she read through the names again.

Disappointment registered all over her face. She didn't make the cut. She turned around to tell her friends and instead came face-to-face with Marisa, Shane, and Brandi. It was tempting to rub it in, but none of them took the opportunity like Ashley would have done had the shoe been on the other foot. "Congratulations," she said somberly to Marisa and Shane.

"Thanks," they both responded, relieved that they wouldn't have to put up with her diva-like attitude.

"Y'all dodged a bullet on that one," Brandi said as they headed over to meet Robin.

"Think Robin's going to leave us again?" Marisa joked half-heartedly as they waited at the front of the school.

"Nah, I think she's climbing out of her funk since the morning sickness has subsided," Shane replied.

"Get in, scrubs!" Robin hollered as she pulled up in front of the school. "Let's eat!"

"Who you calling 'scrub'? I'm the Good Witch of the North. That's what I'll be answering to for the next few months," Shane said, giving her sister the good news.

"Ah, that's great, Shane! I know you really wanted a part in the play. How did it go for you, Marisa?"

Marisa gave her most evil, bewitching laugh to date. "You can call me the Wicked Witch of the West. I'm stoked!"

"Oh, Mari, so sinister. Didn't know you had all that evilness hidden in there," Robin laughed.

It was just like old times. They laughed and sang the rest of the way to Jerry's. Robin seemed to be in a really good mood, and they were all ready to celebrate. Shane told the girls to order and she would pay for it, but Robin refused to let her. "Hey, I owe y'all a dinner, and plus, we are celebrating for you and Mari. You're not going to pay. Now go grab a table."

The girls sat at the table chatting and waiting for their food. Spirits were high, but Brandi seemed more focused on her phone.

"Hey, are you going to come up for air?" Robin asked, trying to snatch Brandi's phone, but she was too quick.

"Nunya! Stay outta my business, woman," Brandi said, moving her phone out of Robin's reach. "I'm on Friender."

"Friender? How much time do you spend on that thing? You are *so* addicted," Shane said, laughing.

"I am not addicted. There's just somebody on here that I've kinda been talking to."

"A boy? Tell me more," Shane said, sounding very intrigued.

"Well, I can show you better than I can tell you." Brandi turned her phone around and revealed a cute-faced, brown boy with chiseled muscles.

"Nice," Marisa said.

"Cutie pie," Shane responded.

"Oh, I get it now, girl, but you be careful with that Internet dating. He could be some fat, bald guy eating potato chips in front of the computer," Robin joked.

"Robin, stop being so negative," Shane told her, knowing that Brandi would probably get annoyed.

"Girl, I'm just joking! Brandi has always known how to pick 'em."

Brandi chimed in, "I made him send me a ton of pictures. There's no way it's not him. He goes to Thurgood Marshall High School, so he's just thirty minutes away. He's too close to try to run a game."

"So, have you met him yet?" Marisa asked.

"Nah, we both have crazy schedules. I don't even know when we would make time to see each other. He's in ninth grade too, so you know he can't drive over here himself."

"Okay … I was joking about the fat dude in front of the computer, but I wasn't joking about being careful. When you meet the dude, just make sure that somebody's with you and it's a public place. Don't fall for all that secretive bull. I've had some friends that got had that way, and it can get ugly," Robin warned her.

"I'm sure it'll be fine. I'll tag along if you need me, B," Shane told her.

"Thank you for all of the wonderful advice, but I think I'll be okay," Brandi said, rolling her eyes at her friends. Friender seemed to be the only place where she could just escape. The excitement of going to her room, turning on her computer, and forgetting all of the problems going on at home was priceless. She was falling in love. Not falling in love with this kid she was talking to, Camden, but falling in love with the anticipation of talking to somebody, the thrill about the secrecy of their relationship, and the ability to lose herself for hours on end in her room. It was easy, and she needed easy. She almost regretted telling her friends about him, but it was something that she really did want to share. She couldn't exactly share what had been going on at home; she wasn't ready for all of that yet.

"Can we just go?" Brandi said, surprisingly annoyed at the conversation. "I need to get home to check on Raven anyway."

"Okay," the girls said, gathering their belongings in awkward silence.

CHAPTER 9

Brandi

Friday night basketball! What could be better? As Brandi slipped on her white home-game uniform, she admired her silhouette in the mirror. She knew she looked good and was ready to cheer at the game. The freshman cheerleaders were relief for the varsity squad at the home games. It was so fun. She loved basketball season. PCH had been state champs for three years in a row, and with the season they were having, they would surely be heading to state again this year.

As soon as she finished putting on her uniform, she added face paint and bows to her hair to give her uniform a little more *oomph*. On cue, Raven knocked on the door. "You ready to go to the game?"

"Girl, you can smell a roll out!" she laughed. "Yes, I'm ready to go to the game, but, Raven, you can't come with me. I have to cheer the entire game. I can't watch you."

"I don't need you to watch me. I'm helping Shane with pictures for the newspaper and yearbook. I have a job to do," she said proudly.

"So does Mom know that Shane is going to be responsible for you and not me?"

Raven looked at her like she was stupid. Even at eight years old, Raven knew that her parents weren't keeping close tabs on them. "B, you know she won't care."

"Hey, don't talk like that. She cares. She just has a lot on her plate."

"You always care," she said, heading to her room to grab her shoes and coat.

A horn blew outside. It was Mrs. Foster. "Bye, Mom! We're leaving!" Brandi yelled as she raced out the door with Raven.

"Okay, girls! Have fun!" her mother yelled back from her bedroom. It was the one place where she could relax and not think about her husband's drug abuse or the extra shifts that she had to pick up at work to make up for his behavior. She just wanted to get lost in her DVR.

As soon as Brandi got to the game, she fell in line with the other cheerleaders. Alexandria Solis, the head cheerleader, led the girls in a warm up. When they entered the gym, the fans were stoked. Brandi scanned the crowds for Raven and spotted her sticking close to Shane.

Then it was time. The girls began their routine. They were on point with a flawless performance. In the final move, Brandi was sent flying through the air in a basket toss that she had been nervous about. But she nailed it.

The crowd erupted. Everyone was ready to watch PCH demolish the visiting team, Semoa High.

The game was close. Semoa was great. But PCH's point guard, Trent, was unstoppable. The boy was on fire. Semoa started hitting three-pointers, catching up fast. Everyone quieted as Semoa tied.

It was do or die. The Semoa fans were going wild. With seconds left, Trent soared through the air, ending the game with a slam dunk. The crowd mobbed the floor. Another PCH victory!

Just as Brandi was congratulating the team, she could feel Raven's hand slip into hers. "That was awesome, Brandi! Totally awesome!" she said, jumping up and down. Shane snapped their picture.

"Hey, don't forget about me," Mari said, appearing from the stands. Shane took another picture, this time with Marisa too.

"Yo, can I get a copy of that?" asked a deep voice.

They turned to see a sweaty Trent towering over them. "Hi, Trent! You know I got you," Shane said.

"Brandi, y'all did good tonight. You got the crowd ready for us."

"Just doing our job, Big T." Brandi smiled.

"I don't believe that we've met," he said to Marisa.

"I don't believe that we have," she responded. "I'm Marisa Maldonado."

"Well, I'm Trent Walker. Nice to meet you. Hey, I gotta run. Coach wants to meet with us. Thanks for the pic, Shane. Hey ... come to think of it ... What are you ladies doing tonight?"

"I think we're going to Jerry's," Shane answered.

"Cool, maybe I'll see you there," he replied, looking more at Marisa than anybody else. And with that, he ran toward the boys' locker room to catch up to the other players.

Marisa looked awestruck.

"You okay?" Shane asked her with a laugh.

"Um ... yeah. He's just so ... tall ... and so ... cute," she said, trying to find her words.

"Okay, well, you work that out," Shane laughed. "I'm going to find my mom."

"Let me get my stuff, and I'll be ready to ride," Brandi said.

"Can I come with you, B?" Raven asked.

"Sure, baby girl. You can come."

Brandi changed her clothes and gathered her things. When she looked at her phone, she had a message on Friender. It read, "You looked beautiful tonight. I was so proud of you when I watched you working the crowd. I can't wait to see you again—C."

Brandi read the message again. She couldn't believe her eyes. Camden had been at the game. *Why didn't he come and talk to me?* she thought. He came all the way to Port City, and she still didn't get to see him in person. That was harsh.

She wrote him back, "Why didn't you come and talk to me? I would have loved to see you too—B."

He responded, "I tried to wait for you after the game, but I lost you in the crowd. My ride was trying to get out of there before the traffic got too bad. I'll try to come to the next game. I promise—C."

Brandi had butterflies in her stomach. He had been so close to her. "Brandi, they're waiting for us. What are you doing?" Raven asked.

"Oh, my bad. I'm ready," she said, giving herself a once-over in the mirror. "Let's go find the girls."

CHAPTER 10

Marisa

When they pulled up at Jerry's, it was packed. Most people were hanging out in the parking lot where the newest Young Dub songs could be heard blaring from the speakers in their cars.

"Oh, girls, it's going down!" Brandi exclaimed. "Everybody's here."

"Hey, don't get too excited. You girls behave like ladies," Mrs. Foster told them. "Call me when you're ready. And not too late. Raven can't be out all night."

"Yes, ma'am," Shane responded to her mother.

Inside there were three registers, so they all lined up at the same time. Just as Marisa was about to pay for her food, she heard a masculine voice say, "I'll get that." It was Trent. He was freshly showered and looking down at her with eyes that made her bones tremble. He had the smoothest brown skin and the whitest teeth that Marisa had ever seen.

"Thank you so much," Marisa said.

"It's my pleasure. You have a table yet?"

"There are no tables. It's standing room only tonight."

"Not for us. They save a couple of booths for the basketball team. Bring your friends. Y'all come sit with us."

Marisa rounded up the girls, and they slid into the reserved booths.

"Yo, Shane, come sit by me," Ashton hollered. He was Trent's best friend.

"What's yo name, chocolate?" one of the guys asked Brandi.

"Yo, y'all need to chill out," Trent said,

laughing. "I'm sorry. They can be animals." Then he whispered into Raven's ear and her face lit up. She nodded her head, and Trent slipped something into her hand.

"Raven, where are you going?" Brandi asked as she ran toward the register. Raven never even looked back. When she returned to the table, she had the biggest ice cream sundae that Jerry's served.

"Girl, you are going to get sick unless you share," Brandi said, laughing.

"Why haven't I seen you before?" Trent whispered to Mari as she tried to nibble on her fries.

"I don't know, Trent. I've been here all year. I've seen you from time to time, but there's always females hanging around trying to get your attention."

"Yeah, it comes along with the territory. People start saying that one day you may go pro, and the groupies find their way to you early. At least that's what my mom keeps telling me."

"Yeah, I can see that. I've never been the type to look for guys with dollar signs in my eyes. I'ma get my own modeling, so I'm not too much worried about somebody else's money. It's all overhyped anyway."

"So now you saying that I'm over-hyped?" he laughed.

"No ... I mean ... not you," she stumbled over her words. She looked up to get some help from Brandi or Shane, but they were laughing and joking with Trent's teammates.

"Hey, it's okay," he said. "You may be the first girl to call me overhyped. Sometimes I think it's a li'l too much too."

"Trent, I really didn't mean it like that."

"I like the way you say my name," he said, changing the subject. She blushed, and played with one of the fries that had now turned cold on her plate. He studied her face. "So a model, huh? I could see that. You are very beautiful."

"You think so?" she asked. She knew

she was beautiful inside and out, but for Trent to say so meant a lot.

"I think beautiful is an understatement. I really want to see you again, Marisa, away from all these people and staring eyes. Can we go out? I want to get to know you."

Her dark brown eyes looked like a doe caught in headlights. "I would like that," she said as she found the strength to look into his eyes. That moment was electric. It was as if they were the only two people in the whole restaurant.

"Let's go get some air." He grabbed Marisa by the hand and stood up.

"Hey, where are you two going?" Ashton asked.

"Just going to get some air. Y'all meet us outside when you're done." He held on to Marisa's hand through the restaurant as the other girls watched in envy. As he opened the door, the coolness of the night rushed at them. When they reached his

Jeep, he turned the heater on and opened up the back.

"Come here," he said. Then he held her in his arms. She could feel the warmth of his body beginning to thaw her cold limbs. Her head was spinning. They were in a parking lot full of people, music, cars, and straight mayhem, yet it seemed that they were the only ones who really mattered. "This is nice," Trent said after what seemed like forever.

"It is," Marisa said, looking up at him. "This is a little bit crazy. Don't you think? I feel like I've known you a lot longer than three hours."

"This is one of those destiny things, girl," he smiled as he looked down at her.

"Hey, cuddle bunnies!" they heard through a sea of noise. Their friends had found them, and reluctantly they loosened their embrace. "What do you two have going on out here?" Shane asked playfully.

"Yeah, y'all in love yet?" Ashton asked Trent.

"Hey, stay in your lane. Don't worry about us. What y'all up to?"

"Nothing but parking lot pimping. Just trying to see who's hot and who's not," one of their friends said.

The team was in rare form tonight. You could see most of them mackin' on females in various areas of the parking lot.

"Dude, throw that Young Dub on," Ashton said.

The mood changed quickly when Young Dub started blaring through the speakers. Everybody in their immediate area started dancing. *Now fall back, fall back, fall back.* They were all singing and dancing like they were at the club. Raven was doing the latest dance moves with an energetic crowd egging her on. "Go, Raven! Go, Raven!" She loved every minute of it.

Just as their parking lot party was in full swing, Shane announced that her mom had just pulled up. "Let's roll," she said.

"Give me a sec," Marisa whispered to Shane. She turned and hugged Trent tightly.

"Too late to call you tonight?" he asked, whispering in her ear.

"No, I'll be up," she said. She ran to catch up to Brandi, Shane, and Raven.

"My girl's in *looove*," Brandi said.

"No, I'm not in love," Marisa said. "I just met him, but there's something special about that one. I just want to figure out what it is."

"I know one thing. He knows how to treat a lady. He bought me an ice cream sundae," Raven announced.

Marisa laughed. "Maybe you're right, Ra-Ra," Marisa said, picking Raven up off the ground in a huge hug and putting her in the tall Tahoe. "Maybe you're right."

"Did you ladies behave?" Mrs. Foster asked once they were all inside.

"Of course we did. Don't we always?" Shane joked.

"You should plead the fifth on that one," Mrs. Foster said, laughing.

Marisa looked out the window. She could still see Trent. The groupies had already started surrounding him, but his eyes were fixed on the black Tahoe as it sped away from Jerry's. Marisa felt butterflies in her stomach. She knew that she had met someone very special, and she wondered where this new road would lead.

CHAPTER 11

Shane

The past few months had flown by and spring break had finally arrived. *The Wizard of Oz* dress rehearsal was scheduled right after school resumed. Shane and Marisa were in her room running lines in between catching up on the soap operas that they had missed.

"I love spring break. Why do we ever have to go back?" Shane asked Marisa.

" 'Cause we would be mad bored if we just sat around watching soap operas and talk shows all day. It takes only so long to see who the real baby daddy is before you go crazy."

"True, true," Shane laughed. "Let's go downstairs and get some lunch. I'm hungry."

"Let's video chat with B first so we can check on her. I've really been thinking about her lately. I don't know why," Marisa told Shane.

"Cool, I miss Raven too. Plus I'm sick of running lines. Maybe they can come over for lunch. It's a beautiful day. We can hang out in the backyard."

They called Brandi on Skype, but Raven answered. "Hey, y'all!" she said cheerfully.

"Hey, Raven! Where's B?" Marisa asked.

"She's in the shower. What are you two up to?"

"We are about to make some lunch and wanted to see if the two of you had already eaten. Can y'all come over?"

"Raven, who are you talking to?" Brandi hollered.

"My other sisters!" Raven called. "They want us to come over for lunch. Can we, B?"

Brandi appeared on the computer. "Hey, BFFs! We can stop by for a little while. I'm meeting Camden tonight at the mall, so I can't be out long. Lunch sounds great, though."

Shane yelled, "Mom! Can you pick Brandi and Raven up?" When her mother didn't respond, she went to go find her.

"So you are going to meet Camden tonight?" Marisa asked Brandi.

"Girl, yes, and I am so nervous. We are just going to catch a movie. We've been talking for so long now. What if he doesn't like me once he sees me?" Brandi asked.

"And that usually happens when? I've never seen a guy not interested in you, so that's a bit of a stretch of the imagination," Marisa said, laughing.

"I just want him to like me. I've been through five outfits and still don't know what to wear ... skinny jeans, dress, tights, wide leg pants ... I don't even know."

"We are on our way!" Shane exclaimed, running back into the room. "And Mom said she'd pick up Buffalo Wild Wings for us."

"Picnic on the patio! Let me throw on some clothes," Brandi said, rushing to disconnect the chat.

True to her word, Mrs. Foster picked up the food, then Brandi and Raven. As soon as they returned to the Foster house, the girls set up a backyard feast. Robin joined the impromptu picnic.

Shane threw on some jams from her iPod, and they sat and ate, enjoying a beautiful Texas spring day. There was nothing like good friends, food, and sunshine.

"Well, I have a doctor's appointment today, so I have to jet. Gavin is supposed to pick me up in thirty minutes," Robin announced. "I'll check y'all later."

"Bye, Robin!" Raven said.

"Peace out, sis!" Shane responded.

"Bye, Robin," Marisa and Brandi said in unison.

Thirty minutes passed, then forty-five. Shane hadn't seen Gavin come to pick up Robin yet. In all the years that Robin and Gavin had dated, he always came in to speak to them. She excused herself from the table and headed upstairs to check on her sister.

"Robin," she said, knocking on the door of her sister's bedroom. "Robin, are you in there?" she asked, trying to turn the doorknob, but it was locked. "Robie, it's me. Open the door." There was still no reply, but the door opened slowly. She could see that her sister had been crying. "What's the matter?" she asked sympathetically.

"He's not even answering the phone. No explanation. No text. Just nothing," she said through her tears.

"Maybe he forgot about your appointment," Shane said.

"No, we spoke earlier. There's really no way he forgot about it. He just doesn't want to go with me, but today is the day of the ultrasound. I don't want to see the baby without him, and I don't want to go alone."

"Are you serious right now?"

"Yes, I'm serious," Robin said defensively. "You can't understand, but—"

"No, I know you're serious, but I also know that you know that you never have to be alone. Mom will bring you to your appointment, and I know a whole slew of people in the backyard who would love to see that little baby. Please, let us come."

"It's too late. I've already missed the ultrasound appointment."

"Oh, please, call them and tell them you were sick. You're always sick anyway."

A small smile lit up Robin's face. "You're right! Go get the girls."

CHAPTER 12

The Baby Factory

They took up an entire section in the waiting room. There were about fifteen doctors at this one facility, so it looked more like a baby factory than a doctors' office. Robin signed the clipboard and took a seat with the girls.

"This place is scary," Marisa whispered as softly as she could.

"Hecks yeah," Brandi said. "I mean, everybody up in here is pregnant."

"Robin Foster," the receptionist called her name, and Robin went to the window. "I need to get a copy of your insurance card." She took Robin's card and stood up to go to the copy machine. She looked as if she was about to give birth any minute.

"Dang! Even the receptionist is pregnant," Shane said, surprised. "I'm not drinking any water up in this place."

"Me neither," Marisa and Brandi declared.

"It's not the water you three dweebs need to be worried about, and stop talking so doggone loud. You're embarrassing," Robin scolded.

"We weren't loud," Shane answered defensively.

"Yeah, right," Robin said. "And stop gawking everyone."

"There are just so many pregnant people all in one place. I've never seen anything like this before," Brandi said.

Robin just stared at them. "Why don't

y'all go and see what they have in the store on the first floor. Grab a snack for Raven."

"Good idea," Marisa said, still a little bit stunned.

"I'll text y'all when it's time to get the ultrasound done," Robin told them.

"Cool. I need some air anyway," Shane declared. They walked outside in virtual silence. That place was a teenager's worst nightmare! As soon as they were back outside in the fresh air and sunshine, Shane let out a cry. "Ugh, my poor sister! That place is crazy."

"I never want to get pregnant," Marisa said, shaking her head. "So many Latinas at our school are trying to make babies. Not me. I'm good. This body is made for modeling, not baby making."

"I'm just never having sex. Just like Robie told us. Never, never, never," Brandi declared.

"Sex? Is that where babies come from?" Raven asked, confused. "That's not what

Mom told me. She said something about some bird."

"No, *mi hija*. Your mom was right," Marisa said, narrowing her eyes at the girls. "Let's go get you a snack from the store."

They knew they had said too much. They all looked at each other sheepishly as they walked back into the building. They headed straight for the small store with shelves lined with candy, cookies, and chips. There was a pickle jar sitting on top of the counter, and a freezer filled with pizzas and other quick bite items that the store's workers could warm up in the microwave. Next to the freezer was the refrigerator with an assortment of drinks.

The store was so small that there was only room inside for them. Anybody else who wanted to come in would have to wait until they were done. Raven quickly found a bag of Funyuns and grabbed a Big Peach soda from the refrigerator. "Done!" she announced.

"I want a pickle," Brandi said. "But I don't want to look like a pregnant chick."

Shane laughed. "Girl, ain't no baby could fit in that flat li'l stomach of yours. Eat the pickle." She turned to the girl behind the counter. "Make that two pickles, please, and two peppermint sticks."

"Now you're talking," Brandi told her, loving the combo.

Marisa chose a bottled water and an orange. They found seats next to the waterfall in the lobby. The running water gave the room a peaceful sound.

"I have to get going. I have my date tonight, and this appointment is taking forever. I thought we'd be out of here by now," Brandi said.

"Can I go with you tonight, B?" Raven asked.

"No, li'l mama. You cannot come on the date with me, but you know that we will do something fantastic tomorrow, so don't worry."

"Hey! That's Robin," Shane said, looking at her phone. "She's up."

When they returned to the waiting room, the nurse was at the door waiting for them. Robin had already been ushered into the room for the ultrasound. She was lying on the table, and the nurse was squeezing some kind of gel onto her stomach. "You ladies are just in time," the nurse said when they walked into the room. She took out a wand and began to spread the gel with it. "Well, look at that."

Robin's head was leaned to the side, looking at the monitor. "That's my baby. Look, Shane," she said with tears forming in her eyes.

"I think it's a girl," Shane said confidently, tearing up.

"Why are we all crying?" Brandi asked.

"I didn't know I would be so emotional," Marisa said through her tears.

"She's my favorite person in the whole wide world," Raven declared.

"Mine too," a masculine voice said from behind them, and there was Gavin looking at the ultrasound image. "I see our babysitters came with you."

"Shut up, Gavin. Where have you been?" Shane said, nudging him in the side. Shane was close to Gavin. He was like a brother to her. He had been in their family for so long. It had been three years since he and Robin had started dating, and now he really was a part of the family.

"Hey, you," he said, looking down at Robin. She was still angry at him, but they could tell that she was softening already.

"Hey," was all Robin said back.

"Robie, we are going to wait in the lobby. Y'all go ahead and finish up the ultrasound," Shane told her. "And you dropping us home," she said to Gavin.

"Yeah, yeah, I know, big head," he said and turned his attention quickly back to the image on the screen.

"*She* is beautiful," Robin said.

"No, *he* is handsome," Gavin retorted.

"Well, I tell you what. The next time we meet up in this room, I'll be able to tell you who's right. How's that?" the nurse asked.

Robin and Gavin looked at each other for the first time as parents. They knew their lives had just changed forever.

CHAPTER 13

Brandi

"Brandi, you look beautiful," Raven said, admiring her sister as she looked at her reflection in the mirror. Brandi wanted to start spring break off right. What better way than to meet up with Camden for their first date?

"Are you sure?" Brandi asked her doubtfully.

"I am positive!" she said.

Brandi wore a pair of skinny jeans, a black tank, a trend-setting black-and-white-striped blazer, and a pair of strappy heels to show off her perfectly pedicured toes. "I mean, I know that I look good, but I don't really know where he's taking me. He said that his brother was going to drop us off, but he wanted to surprise me."

"That sounds like so much fun. So mysterious. I wish I could go with you."

"Maybe next time, baby girl. This is my first time meeting him, and I am nervous enough as it is. I need to do this alone."

"Why does his brother get to come, and I have to stay home?" Raven asked, wounded.

"He's our driver, silly. Can you drive?" she asked, running over to tickle her sister. "Can you drive yet, baby girl?"

"Stop, B, stop!" Raven screamed as her sister tickled her, making her laugh.

"Say uncle!" Brandi yelled.

"No, no ... "

"Say uncle!"

"Okay, okay, uncle, uncle!" Raven hollered, giving in to her big sister.

Brandi stopped tickling her and collapsed on the bed. "Girl, you have me tired. Now you know not to tell Mom and Dad where I'm going, right?" she asked her little sister.

"I know the drill," Raven responded like an obedient soldier. "Plus, I don't even know where you're going."

"Well, don't tell them who I'm going with either. If they ask, just remember I went out with the girls. Dinner and a movie, got it?"

"Got it!"

Brandi's phone alerted her that she had just received a text message. "Hey, that's Camden! They're downstairs. I'm so nervous."

"Don't be nervous. It's going to be fun," Raven said.

Brandi sent Camden a text, "Blow da horn. I'll b by da door." She ran down the stairs and headed toward the kitchen.

Halfway down the hall, she heard the horn blow. "Oh, that's Robin, Mom! I'll see you in a little while."

"Okay, have fun, darling! Do you need any money?" her mom asked, never getting out of bed.

"Nah," she responded, closing the front door behind her. She was so nervous and self-conscious all the way to the car. It was a shiny black Charger. *Nice car*, she thought as she opened the back door and excitedly got in.

"Hey," she said, confused entering the car. "Where's Camden?"

"We have to meet him. He's getting a surprise ready for you, and he didn't want to leave until everything was perfect. I'm Steven, Camden's older brother. It's nice to finally meet you. Camden has told me so much about you."

"He's told me a lot about you too," she said, staring out of the window. She was a little upset. *If Camden wasn't going to show up with his brother, then he should have warned me. I'm glad he's making a fuss over me, but this is not what I had in mind.*

"How about some music? Camden had me download some music for you."

"Well, he's thought of everything, huh?"

"Yeah, that's my little brother for you."

"So, where are we going? He said that we could go to Pappadeaux's 'cause it's my favorite."

"Well, he didn't mention that to me. He just said for me to bring you to him."

Brandi was feeling a bit uneasy about the whole trip. "Where are we going? Are we near the water?" she asked as she talked over the music.

"We're almost there, but I don't want to ruin the surprise," he responded.

"Well, okay. I'll try, but I won't make any promises," she said playfully, attempting to let her defenses down a little.

Steven entered an empty parking garage. The sleek black Charger snaked its way up the side of the building toward the roof. Mirrors lined the walls of the garage so that drivers could see all of the blind spots. Brandi looked out of the window as the car rounded curve after curve. *What a view*, she thought as she watched the waters along the port creep in and out of view.

She could smell the scent of briny water in the air. She was lost in the magic of her whole adventure until they reached the top of the building and the car began to slow to a stop.

"We are here," Steven announced.

"Where is here?" she asked as she exited the vehicle.

"Look over there," he responded. She turned to see white Christmas lights lining the top of the building. It looked beautiful. The coolness of the night air coming across the water added mystery to the evening, and she wanted to see more. "Go on up, have a drink, he'll be out shortly."

She ascended the small staircase that led to where they were going to have dinner. She saw candles and two champagne flutes already filled. She could see the water as she sipped apple cider. *Good choice*, she thought. Last year when she was dating an older guy, he took her to some cheap hotel party where she'd had her first alcoholic drink. She wasn't impressed. She had shared the experience with Camden. *Thank God he's different*, she thought.

Just as she was about to turn around to look for Camden, she started to feel light-headed. Then she felt two hands cover her eyes and pull her in close. She could feel his body against hers. *Finally, he's here.* Briefly she turned around, but it was not Camden's face she saw. Before she could protest, her body went limp and everything went black.

CHAPTER 14

Shane

What an exhausting day, Shane thought as she lowered herself on the bed to watch a little TV. She didn't know what to watch on her DVR: *Real Housewives, Basketball Wives, Football Wives*. Shoot, after a while, it all started to blend together. She decided against all the wives and put on a movie from her collection. She was looking forward to a good night's sleep. She and Marisa were meeting in the morning to run lines for the play.

Shane decided to video chat with

Marisa while she wrapped her hair. "Hey, you! What are you doing?"

"Chillin' with the fam. What about you?"

"I'm about to watch a movie and chill so I'll be fresh for tomorrow. Have you heard from B?" Shane asked.

"No, not yet. I hope she likes this Camden dude. I'd hate for her to be disappointed."

"Yeah, me too. I know she was all into this one."

"Well, you know our girl. When she falls, she falls hard," Marisa said.

"Yeah, she does. Especially now. There's something going on with her family, and she's looking for comfort right now."

"I know. I just hope she finds it."

"Yeah, me too. You know I'm protective when it comes to my girls," Shane declared.

Marisa laughed. "And we love you too!"

"Okay, I'm fully wrapped and prepared to watch *B.A.P.S.*"

"Tell me you're not watching *B.A.P.S* again!"

"Now you know I have to get my Halle Berry on at least once a month," Shane declared.

"You are the only person I know who watches *B.A.P.S*," she said, shaking her head. "Well, let me get back to game night before they start calling me."

"A'ight, late!" Shane said.

"Late! See you in the morning," Marisa responded.

Shane pressed play on the remote. Not wanting to interrupt the movie, she ignored her ringing phone that was plugged in across the room. "Halle Berry is hilarious. That girl straight up dumb for accepting this part," she said, laughing as Halle Berry danced, showing off her fake gold tooth and extra large booty.

Thirty minutes later the house phone began to ring. *Ain't nobody answering a house phone in this day and age*, she thought. *Who could that be at midnight anyway?* She didn't give it another thought as she finished the movie and curled up under her covers.

Lord, I forgot to call B. She sat up in bed and headed to take her phone off the charger. When she looked at the phone, she realized that her missed call was from Brandi's house. Why didn't she just call from her cell? *It's too late to call on the house phone now,* she thought. She dialed Brandi's cell, but it went straight to voice-mail. *She must be asleep. I'll catch her in the morning.* And with that, she went to bed.

CHAPTER 15

Marisa

*A*s soon as Marisa hung up with Shane, she went back into the living room where her family was playing Connect Four. "Let's play something that we can all play," she declared as she joined her family.

"It's six of us, *mi hija*. What would you suggest?" her father asked.

"Monopoly, of course. It's the only thing that we can all play," Marisa responded. Her two sisters didn't have a problem with Monopoly, but her little brother, Romero, always put up a fuss. At twelve years old, Monopoly was way too long for him.

"I ain't playin' Monopoly," he declared.

She leaned over and whispered, "Come on, Rom. Do it for me."

"Okay, Mari," he said. He would do anything for Marisa.

Monopoly in their family could take all night because they played by the rules. Both of her sisters had already gone bankrupt by eleven and were downloading music on the computer. Her mom and dad were both yawning, but they could see that the end of the game was nearing. Marisa snuck some money to Romero to keep him in the game, but he was getting tired too. She could hear her cell phone ringing in the other room. She looked at the wall clock. *Eleven thirty-five? Who would be calling so late?* she wondered.

Romero looked at his sister. "Your phone's ringing," he said.

"Yeah, I know. I'm only waiting on one call, and my girls have their own ring. I know it's not them. I'll check after the game."

"But it could be Trent," he said, teasing her.

"He has his own ring too. Now stay out of my business," she said, hitting him with a pillow.

By midnight, her father had successfully taken everybody's money and property. They were putting the game away, stretching, and getting ready to go to bed.

Before Marisa took her shower and headed to bed, she made sure to send Brandi a text, "How wuz ur date?"

She received back, "Gr8 cant wait to tell u bout it. Wil cal u 2morow so tired gn."

She jumped in the shower and let the water wash away the day. Showers were one of her favorite pastimes. The water was so loud that it drowned out any noise in the house, and she could focus on her own thoughts. *Me time. I love it*, she thought.

As she washed her hair, her mind drifted to all of the things that she had going on in her life. She pictured herself on stage in front of the whole school and envisioned the standing ovation that she would get when she took her bow after the play. She saw herself as she walked runways in New York, Paris, Milan. She pictured her dream home. She knew that if she was going to be successful she had to picture it first.

She got out of the shower, wiped the mirror, and looked back at the young woman looking at her. "You can do this," she said, encouraging her reflection to keep pushing toward her dreams. A small town Texas girl from Port City. The odds were definitely not in her favor, but she knew that she could do great things. She just had to keep pushing.

By the time she was ready for bed, it was almost one. "No wonder I'm tired," she said out loud. She wanted to try to catch up with B, but it was too late, even for them. *Why didn't she call me when she got home?* she wondered.

Marisa quickly fell asleep, but shortly thereafter, there was a knock on the front door. Her room was located in the front of the house, so she was usually the first person to know if company was coming to visit. She was always the first to greet her *abuelita* when she arrived for the holidays, and the first to know when the pizza delivery man was at the door. Tonight she would be the first person to be awakened by Mrs. Haywood.

CHAPTER 16

Missing

Raven had been tossing and turning, waiting for Brandi to get home. She wanted to hear about her date with Camden. But her sister never arrived.

The person who entered her room was her mom. It was nearly midnight. "Ra-Ra, are you awake?" she asked.

Raven lay there with her back to her mother. She didn't answer, but her mother didn't leave. "Ra-Ra, wake up, honey," her mother said gently.

"Huh?" Raven asked, trying to pretend she was asleep so that she wouldn't have to answer a bunch of questions. She was not about to get her sister in trouble. *No way, no how*, she thought.

"Have you heard from your sister?" her mother asked her.

"No, ma'am," Raven answered.

"Did she say where she was going with the girls? I've been trying to call them, but I can't reach anybody."

"She said they were going to dinner and a movie. That's all I know," Raven said, sticking to the script.

"Well, that doesn't take until after midnight. What did they go see?" she asked, still quizzing her youngest daughter.

"I don't know, Mom," Raven hollered, crying. "Just leave me alone," she said as she turned over in her bed.

"Raven," her mother said sternly, "what are you not telling me?" She flicked the light on to get a better look at her daughter.

Raven squinted under the bright light. "Mom," she whined. "What are you doing?"

"I'm trying to get some answers. You've never been good at keeping secrets, so spill it. It's after midnight, and I'm not playing any games with you."

Raven began to cry again. She hung her head. She just didn't want to get her sister in trouble. Mrs. Haywood reached out to comfort her daughter. "Baby, what's going on here? You're starting to scare me."

"She's not with the girls, Mom," Raven said nervously.

"What ... what do you mean?"

"She went out on a date ... with this guy," Raven admitted.

"Get in the car. Get in the car now!" her mother yelled. Leaving Raven home with her father wasn't an option. Having one daughter missing was enough for Mrs. Haywood. She drove straight to the Fosters' home. It was the closest, and she knew that Shane would know what was going on.

"Cat? Is that you? What's going on? It's nearly one o'clock in the morning," Mrs.

Foster said, letting Catherine Haywood and a visibly scared Raven into the house.

"I'm looking for Brandi, Kim. She's not at home. She told me she was going out with Shane and that Robin was driving. I didn't know where else to go. I tried to call you. I'm so sorry to wake you up," she said apologetically.

"No problem. Are you sure she's not just running late?"

"You know, I don't know. That may be the case, but for some reason, I feel like something is wrong. I just can't shake it."

"A mother's intuition ... " Mrs. Foster's voice trailed off.

"Do you think I can talk to Shane for a minute? Maybe she knows something."

"Sure. Let me get her," Mrs. Foster said, leaving to wake her youngest daughter.

Shane appeared at the bottom of the stairs looking as if she was five years old and had been caught playing with her mom's makeup. "Hi, Mrs. Haywood."

Catherine stared at her daughter's best friend. "Brandi hasn't come home. Do you know where my baby is?" Mrs. Haywood asked with tears on her face.

"No, ma'am. I don't know," she said, still looking at the ground.

"Well, does Marisa know? Have you talked to her?"

"Mrs. Haywood," Shane said, starting to cry. She knew that they had pooh-poohed Robin's assertion that this online chatting thing was a bad idea. But she had told Brandi to be careful and now look.

"What, Shane? Tell me. Brandi could be in serious trouble."

"Baby, you have to be honest right now," Shane's mother said.

"The boy's name is Camden. B met him on Friender a while back. We tried to warn her about dating dudes from the Internet, but she just wouldn't listen. Tonight was supposed to be their first date."

Brandi's mother froze. Mrs. Foster grabbed her hand and yelled for her husband. "Honey, get up! We have to call the police. Brandi's missing."

Mrs. Haywood shook herself from her shock. She turned to Mrs. Foster. "Kimberly, can I borrow Shane? Maybe she can help me get to the bottom of this."

"Of course. Anything you need, please don't hesitate to call. I'll keep my phone close."

"Thanks," she said, darting out of the house with Raven and Shane.

"Where are we going?" Shane asked as she jumped in the car with Mrs. Haywood.

"First, we are going to talk to Marisa. Then ... then hopefully the police will know something."

They arrived at the Maldonado home a little after one in the morning. Mrs. Haywood knocked hard enough to wake the whole house, but it was Marisa who came to the door. She looked angry, but when she saw the disheveled Mrs. Haywood, her anger turned to concern.

"Mrs. Haywood? What are you doing here?" Marisa asked. She didn't even notice the two figures standing behind her on the dark porch until she flipped on the porch light. "Shane?" she asked. "What's go—"

"Have you heard from Brandi?" Mrs. Haywood asked, cutting her off.

"Yeah, I did. I sent her a text and she replied back. It was just after midnight. She said that she was tired and would call me in the morning."

"Did she say where she was?"

"No, I just assumed she was at home," Marisa responded, growing increasingly alarmed. "Did you check her room? I could swear—"

"She's not in her room, Mari," Shane said, tears streaming down her face.

"What do you mean? I'm confused. She never made it back home?"

"No, baby, we haven't heard from her," Mrs. Haywood said, lowering her head.

"Let me throw some clothes on and tell my parents what's going on. I need three minutes," Marisa said, dashing away from the door. She grabbed clothes to change into, told her confused parents what was happening, and threw herself in Mrs. Haywood's Acura.

They rode in virtual silence all the way to the Haywood home. There were already three cop cars outside. Two of the officers were inside gathering pictures and a description of Brandi from Mr. Haywood. It was as if they had walked into a dream.

CHAPTER 17

Brandi

"Where? What?" Brandi said out loud, feeling confused and dizzy. She tried to move her tired arms but she couldn't. *Where am I?* she wondered. She tried to wrap her mind around what happened the night before. *I went out with Camden. Wait ... I never saw Camden, but there were lights and decorations and then ... I don't know. I don't know. Oh my God! Oh my God!* She began to panic.

"Hello?!" she screamed. "Where am I? How long have I been here?" Tears were beginning to form in her eyes. She had to be strong. She fought the tears away. Now was not the time to cry. She had to clear her mind so that she could get out of here. She was sitting in a chair, and she struggled to free herself from the ropes that bound her to it.

The more she tried to undo the ropes, the tighter they became. They began to cut into her flesh and burn her arms. The ropes on her ankles were actually causing her to bleed. She had unknowingly been putting more pressure on the ropes that bound her ankles. Then panic started to take over, and she began to cry. She was feeling hopeless.

There was no sound in this cold, damp little room. There was one sad lamp that sat on a stand in the corner. On the other side of the room was a small pillow and blanket that was used on airplanes for the passengers. The floor was hardwood and made the room feel even colder. Brandi surveyed the room and became even more frightened. *What's happening to me?* she wondered.

She sat in that chair for what seemed like hours. There was no movement anywhere. She listened intently for clues about where she was, but there was no sound. She put her head down and thought. She tried to recall every conversation with Camden. She tried to remember everything about his brother. She had to figure out why he would have done this.

She had never talked to him on video chat like most people did these days. Instead he would just send pictures of himself. He said that the camera on his computer was out. *Why did I believe that?* She beat herself up thinking of all the mistakes she had made.

Once, her computer teacher had a guy come speak to them about the dangers of the Internet. She listened intently that day. She even took notes about looking for warning signs of predators, and she knew that she was way too street smart to be fooled like that. "He's going to have to wake up early in the morning to try that mess with me," she had boasted, dapping up one of her friends. And now here she sat in this room, hands and feet both bound to a hard wooden chair that made her back ache.

Just when she was about to doze off, she heard a sound outside of the door. "Hello? Is somebody there? Help me, help me please!" she screamed. *"Ayudame por favor!"* she even tried saying it in Spanish. She could be anywhere at this point. She wasn't leaving any bases uncovered.

The door opened slowly and Camden's brother entered the room. He didn't say anything. He put a small bag of food on the floor next to the pillow and blanket. Then he laid an outfit down on top of the covers. Brandi immediately recognized the clothing as her own. "How did you?

That's my stuff!" she yelled, but Steven never said a word. Confusion clouded her mind. *How did he get my clothes? Who is this guy?* She squinted her eyes, trying to make out his face. He looked really familiar. She knew she'd seen him before. But where? And why didn't she notice this last night?

He walked closer to her and pulled a knife from his pocket. Brandi's body tensed. She didn't know what was about to happen, but she couldn't show any signs of weakness, so she braced herself. He came closer to her, and the closer he came, the closer the knife came. She could smell his cologne as it invaded her space, and she felt like vomiting. He put the knife to her throat without saying a word. He looked deep into her eyes and let the knife follow down the silhouette of her body without cutting her. She could feel the cold, sharp blade against her arm, through her jeans and then to her ankle.

He cut the ropes around her ankles and surveyed the damage they left behind; he was pleased. He gently examined her cuts and bruises. He was in no rush. He untied both legs and looked up at her. In a low, menacing voice he said, "Don't even think about running, or I'll kill you."

He then took the knife and cut the ropes that bound her arms. As soon as her arms and legs were free, she immediately lunged at him. She knew that he wouldn't think she would be so brave, not at that moment. She wanted to surprise him, catch him off guard. She clawed and scratched at his face and eyes until he was forced to drop the knife, but he came back at her with a blow so strong that it sent her small body flying against the wall.

"Next time, I won't be so nice," he said, picking up the knife and pointing it at her. "Now eat your food and change your clothes," he demanded. "I'll be back to see you soon."

Brandi cowered in the corner listening to the words of her captor. She had failed. She was scared and cold. She thought of her mother and father and Raven. They were probably looking for her everywhere. She was sure they were scared. She had told Raven not to tell, but she prayed to God she had. How could she have done this to her family?

Just when she thought that things couldn't get any worse, the one little light in the corner of the room went black. She sat in there in darkness. Her hands searched for the small pillow and blanket that lay somewhere close to her on the floor. Her fingers found the softness of them both. She pulled the pillow and blanket close to her body as if they could somehow protect her, but she could smell his scent on both of them. *Ugh!* That's when she lost it. There was no comfort here. Nothing could protect her from this monster. She sat there rocking, sometimes screaming for help. She cried for hours, until it seemed that there were no more tears. When she was too exhausted to cry, the only thing left to do was sleep. Her body lay limp and tired on the cold floor. She had never felt so helpless.

CHAPTER 18

Marisa

The ringing of Marisa's alarm clock awakened her from another torturous night. It was the first day back to class following spring break—the first day back to school since Brandi's disappearance. *This has to be some sort of nightmare*, she thought to herself. She looked at her phone. No calls from Brandi. It was real. Her best friend was gone.

Marisa hurriedly got dressed and headed for the bus stop. She really had no desire to go to school today, but she did. She couldn't miss. Today was the first day of play practice, and that was the one thing that she could control right now.

Her mind was somewhere else as she took the all too familiar walk to the bus stop. There was a car lingering in the distance that she never noticed. The car made a U-turn and crept up behind her. She heard a window roll down. "Excuse me, miss," a voice said.

Marisa turned abruptly to tell the guy to beat it. She wasn't in the mood. When she looked into the car to give them her best *Don't-even-try-it* look, she locked eyes with Trent Walker. He was holding a Starbucks cup in his hand and had a huge smile on his face. A small smile crept to Marisa's lips, and she got into the passenger side of his Jeep.

"Thought you might want some company this morning. I know this must be a hard day for you," he said gently, looking at her in between watching the road.

"Yeah," she answered as she sipped her coffee. "You have no idea."

"You're right. I don't," he answered. Trent put on some music so they wouldn't have to just focus on the negative. They passed a digital billboard with an Amber Alert:

Child Abduction: 14-year-old
5' 1" / brown hair / brown eyes
Last seen wearing jeans and
black-and-white striped jacket
Dial 911 with information

One lone tear fell from Marisa's eyes. Trent reached over and wiped it away. She had almost forgotten where she was or who she was with. It had already been a difficult day, and it had barely begun.

"Hey, thanks for picking me up," she said to Trent. "And for the cappuccino."

"It was my pleasure. Tomorrow I'll just pick you up from your house, though. The weather report said we have a fifty percent chance of rain," he said bashfully.

"I'd like that," she said, returning his bashful gaze. The two of them were at the beginning of their relationship and unsure about how the other felt. They both had a feeling that this was something special, but with everything going on in Marisa's life, she had no choice but to take it slow.

CHAPTER 19

Shane

As Shane entered the gates lined with missing person posters of her best friend, she felt as if she were in some bad dream. The atmosphere looked different. *Where are you, B?* she asked over and over in her head. *Where are you?*

When she walked in the building, she went straight to Mrs. Monroe's classroom. She wasn't there. Shane sat down and looked out the window. Her mind was fixated on the posters. She knew every detail of Brandi's picture. She was the one who had taken it. They had cropped it so her face was close up, but you could still see Port City High in the background.

"Shane?" Mrs. Monroe said, standing at the classroom door.

"Oh, hey, Mrs. Monroe. How was your spring break?" Shane asked, trying not to sound too vulnerable, but Mrs. Monroe could tell that she was.

"It wasn't so great. On the way back from Galveston, I was greeted with Amber Alerts about Brandi. I just lost it," she said.

Shane's head fell to her chest. "How am I supposed to make it through the day, Mrs. Monroe?" she asked, shaking her head. "I couldn't even go to my locker. I knew she wouldn't be there."

Mrs. Monroe walked over to the desk where Shane sat and gently rubbed her back. "It won't be easy, baby, but you can do it. I know you can."

Just then, they heard the bell ring, signaling the start of the school day. Shane wiped her tears and got ready to face the crowds of people. They all looked at her with sorrow in their eyes. Some people whispered as she passed. She could hear them say, "That's her. That was her best friend." She was getting angrier and angrier. *Why are they talking about her like she's dead? That* was *her best friend?!*

She ran to the restroom. She didn't know what else to do. She heard the door to the restroom open behind her, but there were no footsteps. *I just want to be alone!* She spun around with fire in her eyes, but the person that she saw stood there looking helpless and pitiful. It was Marisa.

"They keep talking about her like she's dead, Shane," Marisa said through her tears.

They held each other and cried. Then they heard their names over the intercom. They were being summoned to the principal's office. They pulled away from each other and looked in the mirror. "Oh snap!" Shane said.

"Yeah, me too," Marisa responded. They looked a mess. The eyeliner and mascara that had been so carefully applied that morning was running down their faces. The blush had been smeared and the lip gloss was nonexistent. They tried to pull it together, but when they left the restroom, it was obvious that they had been crying. At least they were able to get most of the smeared makeup off.

When they arrived in the office, there were girls from the cheerleading squad already sitting in the chairs. The first person who stood up was Christina. She was Brandi's closest friend on the squad and Marisa and Shane knew it. "I'm so sorry that this happened," she said. They could tell that she had been crying too. Shane reached out and hugged her.

"They'll find her, Christina. I just know they will," Shane said.

The captain of the cheerleading squad,

Alexandria, held tightly to Marisa's hand as they stood close to Christina and Shane.

All of Brandi's closest friends had already been questioned the days after her abduction. She had gone missing the Tuesday during the break, and by Thursday they had all been summoned to the police station and questioned extensively. This was something different, though. A grief counselor had been called in to speak with them about the ordeal, and to help them adjust to getting back to their routines.

"Follow me, ladies," the female counselor led them to a small room on the side of the main office.

None of them had ever been in this room before. There was a large circular table for them to sit. The counselor introduced herself to the girls. "My name is Linda Thibodeaux. You can call me Ms. Linda. The only thing that I know about you young ladies is that each of you loves Brandi. I know that this has been a hard week for you, and I just wanted to let you all know that I will be on campus as long as you need me here. If you need anything, then you can just knock on my door. If it's after hours, here's my card. You can always call me. Is there anything that we need to address right now? Any concerns?"

"Why do people keep talking about her in past tense? Why do they talk about her like she's dead?" Shane asked. "It's only been five days."

"We can't control what other people think or say. They don't know Brandi the way that you ladies do. Just stay hopeful and don't let anybody bring you down."

"No offense Ms ... " Shane paused.

"Ms. Linda."

"Ms. Linda, but you don't know Brandi either," she finished. "How are we supposed to confide in somebody who doesn't even understand what we are going through?

You don't know her, and you don't know me. This is stupid," Shane said and stood up to walk out of the door.

"Shane," Marisa called out after her, but she didn't slow down. "Sorry, Ms. Linda. She's just upset," Marisa said, chasing Shane out of the office. "Shane, Shane," she yelled, watching as Shane ran out of the front door of the school.

Marisa chased after Shane. They were both in a bad place, but it had always been hard for Shane to deal with stress. After all, it had only been a few months since Shane had overcome abusing Adderall and weed. Marisa knew that she shouldn't be alone.

"Stop, Shane, please," she said.

Shane stopped dead in her tracks and turned to look at her best friend. "I don't work without B," she yelled, tears streaming down her face.

"I don't either," Marisa said, her own eyes filling up with tears.

Looking at all of the posters with Brandi's face lining the fence surrounding the courtyard, they held tightly to each other under a big oak tree in the front of the school. "Dear God, bring Brandi home," was all Shane had the energy to say.

CHAPTER 20

No Stone Unturned

Marisa and Shane arrived at the Haywood home as they had done every day after school since Brandi had gone missing. It seemed the only place where they could feel close to her. Raven needed them. Her parents needed them, and they needed the Haywoods. It had been exactly twenty days since they had seen Brandi. They seemed to be the only people in town who still believed that she would be found alive.

"Hey, Mrs. Haywood," Shane said as Catherine Haywood opened the door to let the girls into the house.

"Hi, ladies. How was your day at school?" she asked.

"It was okay," Marisa answered uncomfortably. They all knew that their days would only start to be good again once Brandi was home.

"Ra-Ra, we see you at the top of the stairs. Come down, okay?" Shane asked. Raven didn't reply.

"We're going to go talk to her, Mrs. Haywood. We'll be in Brandi's room," Marisa said. Marisa scooped Raven up in her arms when she got to the top of the stairs and carried her to the room. "You're getting too big for this, squirt," she said, dropping Raven in the middle of the massive pillows on Brandi's bed and cuddling up next to her.

Raven sank her face into Marisa's arm. She hid there without saying a word.

Shane walked over to the bed and sat next to them, rubbing Raven's back.

"Hey," she said in a low whisper. "We are going to get her back. You know that B is strong. She'll be home in no time. When she gets back, she's going to need you. You have to stay strong, Raven," she pleaded. "You just have to, baby girl."

Raven began to cry. "It's all my fault. I should have told my mom. I should have known that this was a bad idea."

Marisa pulled away from her, forcing Raven to look at her. She looked her square in the eyes. "It is *not* your fault. We all knew that Brandi had a date with this guy. We even told her that we would go with her. She made the decision, not you. Don't blame yourself. There's no way that any of us could have known, not even Brandi herself."

Raven cried and again buried her head in Marisa's arm. It was going to take more than one conversation for Raven to believe that she wasn't the cause of her sister's disappearance.

"Come on, baby girl. We have to get back to work," she urged Raven. In the days that Brandi was gone, they had tried to piece together anything they could on Camden. They took out their notes, their timelines, and their computers.

"Camden stopped updating his Friender page on the day Brandi went missing," Shane said.

"He'd been planning the kidnapping all along. No way he's a ninth grader. But who is he?" Marisa asked.

"That's what we need to figure out," Shane said.

A loud engine revved outside. Raven rushed to the window. "Shoot," she said, sinking into a chair.

"What?" Shane asked.

Raven looked at the floor.

"Raven, talk to us. Is there something going on?" Marisa asked gently.

"I told my mom, and she doesn't believe me. You probably won't either," Raven said sadly.

"Try us," Shane urged.

"Well, I was peeking out the window the night Brandi disappeared. I saw Camden's car. I told the police about it, but they didn't say much."

"What's crazy about that?" Marisa asked. She gave Raven's arm a squeeze.

"The thing is, I think I hear that car every day. It drives by the house, slows down, then speeds away. I only see the back lights." Raven sighed. "I don't know. I guess it sounds crazy."

"Ra-Ra, that's not crazy," said Marisa.

"I'm going to add it to the logbook. If you think that you are hearing something, then we are going to look into it. No stone unturned, right?" Shane said to Raven.

"Thanks, Shane, for taking me serious. Mom thought I was being silly," she confided in the girls.

"Well, we don't. At this point nothing's silly," Marisa told her.

They all held hands and prayed for Brandi to come home.

CHAPTER 21

Brandi

There was no way of knowing how long she had been in this room. She tried to count the number of meals that she had eaten, the number of times that he had allowed her to go to the restroom. He seemed to bring meals to her once a day. She knew at least two months had gone by, but she'd lost count after day sixty. It seemed as though she had been here forever. At times she wondered if she would ever leave this dark little room, but she pushed those thoughts away and tried to stay hopeful.

The lamp that once lit the room hadn't worked since the first day. In the beginning, she would ask him to bring a light so she could see, but he wouldn't respond. He didn't like to talk much, and he seemed to prefer the dark. When he came around, he moved through the darkness like a cockroach that knew exactly what it was after.

He never stayed long. But she tried to draw him out. She knew that deep down he had buried the person who had intrigued her so much on Friender.

Mostly she just sat in the corner, thinking. Sometimes she would get up and do jumping jacks to stay active.

She had the chance to study him. He looked like an average guy. Dark brown skin, nice manicured eyebrows. He didn't look like a kidnapper. But his eyes seemed empty.

"Hey," she said as he entered the room. She was trying to warm up to him. She wasn't afraid of him anymore. He hadn't laid a hand on her, and it didn't seem that he wanted to. If he had wanted to harm her, he could have done so countless times. "Steven?" she said, trying to get him to look at her before he shut the door and there was no more light. But he avoided eye contact in those brief moments of light.

He closed the door and handed her a bag. She felt inside and grabbed a sandwich. She followed his silhouette as he moved through the small room. He went to the wall and plugged in a small light. Brandi frowned as the light stung her eyes.

"Steven, can I ask you something?" He looked at her in the dim light. She took this as a cue to go on. "When we used to talk on the computer, you were so interesting and funny. Now you don't talk to me at all. Why?" she asked, attempting to flatter him.

"I don't like to talk," he responded dryly.

"But you like to chat on the computer? What's the difference?" She couldn't get him to respond. He just stared at his feet as he sat next to her.

"Why am I here, Steven?" she pleaded. "Tell me. You know my family is probably scared to death. When are you going to let me go? My little sister ... I'm all she has," she said as she started to cry. This was not a part of her plan. She had lost focus.

"Raven is fine," he said definitively.

She looked at him. "How do you know?" she asked, obviously shocked that he had even mentioned her little sister's name. Had he been stalking her sister too? This was way too much for Brandi to comprehend. "How do you know?" she screamed at him, trying to get him to make eye contact.

It was all too much for him. He became noticeably shaken. He had to make a quick exit. He headed straight for the door but stopped cold in his tracks. He turned back to the wall and yanked the only source of light Brandi had had for weeks from the outlet. The room went black, and he was gone.

"Noooo," she screamed as he left her again. "No," she said as her defeated body slid down the wall. She couldn't believe that this was happening. "Raven," she cried.

When he returned the next day, Brandi hadn't moved. She was so upset. She couldn't move. Even when he plugged the small nightlight into the wall, she didn't respond. He had won. There was nothing that she could do to help herself. All she could do was wait for some kind of divine intervention.

He threw another outfit down next to her, skinny jeans and a white tank top. "Put this on," he said, turning his back.

"What the—" these were her clothes too. *How is this guy getting my stuff? This is too weird.* She tried to remain calm and not overreact.

He unlocked the bathroom door so she could freshen up. "Leave the door open," he demanded. She was afraid that he would watch her, but he turned his back. She took the brush and rubber band that he brought to her and combed through the tangled mess of hair on her head as best she could. She fastened the rubber band tightly around the ponytail. It was the best she could do. She used her finger as a toothbrush. There was no mirror. She wondered if her eyes showed the terror she was feeling.

"I'm done," she announced.

"Here, eat," he commanded, handing her a turkey sandwich on white bread. "I have a drink for you too."

Brandi at the sandwich slowly. The drink felt so good going down. It reminded her of Kool-Aid. Before long, she became very relaxed. "What did you put in my drink?" she asked, but her speech was slurred. She started to become frightened.

"I just gave you something to calm you down. We are going to take a little ride. You do want to get out of here, right?" he asked, knowing the answer.

She nodded her head. It was the only gesture she could muster. He took out a blindfold and covered her eyes. He tried to guide her from the room, but the drug he had given her really didn't allow her to walk, so he lifted her in his arms. Brandi rested her head against her captor's chest while he carried her to a car. Once he placed her in the passenger's side, she heard a garage door go up and the car backed out.

With the blindfold still in place and the drugs working on her, she soon dozed off. After driving for what seemed like an hour—but was actually fifteen minutes—Steven removed the blindfold from Brandi's face. Her eyes tried to adjust. She thought she was hallucinating. She blinked. She was on her own street. She was home.

Steven pulled the car into a spot across the street from Brandi's house. She didn't know what to say. *Is he letting me go home now?* she wondered. Her thoughts were interrupted when a bus slowly stopped in front of her home. It was Raven's bus. When it pulled away, she was standing there in the driveway. She looked smaller and sadder than Brandi had remembered. Raven's eyes went straight to their car, almost like she could feel Brandi there. Her eyes seemed to meet Brandi's through the dark tinted windows. Steven became nervous and sped away.

"What are you doing?" she tried to scream, but the drugs that he gave to her didn't allow her to. Her voice was full of panic despite being weak. "Let me out right now. Let me out of this car."

She tried to get out of the car, but the door wouldn't budge. Steven's cool demeanor let her know that he was in control. As the car moved further away from the house, a feeling of defeat fell over Brandi. "I want to go home, Steven. I just want to go home," she sobbed, leaning her head against the door. Her head was spinning. Tears streamed down her face. She had been so close to home, Raven, her life. But just like that, it was snatched away.

CHAPTER 22

Shane

*H*ey, do you know which scenes they are running through today?" Shane asked Marisa when she showed up at her locker.

"They posted it on Friender. Let me pull it up now," Marisa responded.

"I should have thought of that myself. Too much on my mind, I guess." As Shane finished putting the contents of her backpack into her locker, she could feel her phone vibrating in her purse. It was Raven. "Hey, Ra-Ra," she said, trying to sound upbeat. "Wait ... calm down ... what did you just say?" she asked.

"What?" Marisa nudged her. She could tell that something was wrong. Her mind went straight to Brandi. She felt her panic level rising.

"But that's not possible. Okay ... okay ... no don't say that. I believe you. Let's talk when we get there."

"What's happening?" Marisa whispered to Shane, who didn't seem to be paying attention.

"We are on our way!" Shane said into the phone.

"What ... what's going on?" Marisa questioned.

"It's Raven. She says that she just saw Brandi."

"But how's that possible?" Marisa asked her.

"I don't know, but we have to hear her out. She was afraid that nobody would believe her."

"Poor Raven. This has been a lot for her. I'll call Trent. He can bring us over there."

"Please tell him to hurry. She sounds really upset."

Marisa made the call to Trent. He and Ashton showed up in the student parking lot within minutes. They both looked as if they had been working out. Marisa felt bad for interrupting basketball practice.

"I'm sorry to bother y'all. Were you at practice?" she asked.

"Nah, it was canceled today. Coach's wife is having her baby, so we were just working out."

"Let's get going. You didn't hear how upset Raven was," Shane said to Marisa.

"I'm sure it's nothing, but she's been through so much," Marisa told Trent as they piled into his car.

"No worries. I'm glad we could help."

"And I'm always down for a roll out. Plus, I'm the muscle," Ashton declared. "If things gotta get ugly, I'm your man." Ashton could make anything sound funny.

He was always joking and clowning. Just his presence could lighten a mood.

They pulled up at the Haywood home, and Raven was sitting outside on the porch. As soon as she saw Shane and Marisa, she ran to the car.

"I saw Brandi," she started talking rapidly. "She was in that car. The black car that I told you about ... I know it was her." Raven's eyes started to fill up with tears.

"Slow down, Ra-Ra," Shane told her. "Tell me what happened."

"Well, I was on the bus, staring out the window. I look for that car everywhere. So when the bus pulled up, I thought I saw it parked across the street. When the bus pulled away, I could see better. And there she was. She looked so pitiful. She saw me see her too." Raven started to cry. "He drove off with her. He just drove off," she said between tears.

"I'm calling the police," Shane said. "They need to get to the bottom of this."

"Wait," Marisa said, pulling Shane to the side.

"For what? If Raven saw Brandi, then they need to know." Shane was determined.

While she was on the phone, Marisa held Raven as they all waited outside. The police arrived about twenty minutes later. By this time, Shane was livid. "What took you so long?" she asked one officer.

"Ma'am, we got here as soon as we could. What seems to be the problem?"

Shane looked down at Raven. "Tell them what you told us," she said.

Raven looked at the ground. She didn't think that they would believe her. She started to tell the story about the black car and seeing her sister. As she was talking to the officer, Mrs. Haywood drove up. She jumped out of the car in a panic, "What's happened? Is it Brandi? Oh my God."

"No, ma'am," the officer replied. "Can I talk to you for a moment in private."

"Sure," Mrs. Haywood said.

They walked out of earshot of the girls. "I think that your youngest daughter needs a lot of support right now. She says that she sees a black car all the time that looks like the one Brandi was last seen in. Now she claims that she saw her sister today in that same car. This just doesn't sound likely."

Mrs. Haywood fussed with her hands. "This has been hard on all of us. I'm just sorry that they called you out here for that."

"It's no problem, ma'am. Anything that we can do to help." The officer walked back over to Raven. "We are going to do everything we can to find your sister," he said.

"You have to find that black car," Shane said.

Mrs. Haywood stepped in. "Shane, they are working on that."

"Then they should work harder," she grumbled, growing more and more agitated. "If Raven says that car is on this street every day, then set up surveillance.

Do something. Isn't that what they get paid to do?" Shane asked, visibly shaking at this point.

Marisa walked over to her. "Hey, relax," she said.

"I will not relax until Brandi's home. And I won't let them relax either."

"I'm going to do my best," the officer said. "But I have to admit, when someone goes missing, they aren't usually sitting in a car across from their home."

"I know what I saw," Raven screamed and ran toward the house. "You have to believe me."

"I know she's only eight, but Raven is a smart girl, Officer," Shane said. "Please, we need your help."

"I will do what I can," he said. "Mrs. Haywood, again, call if you need anything."

"Thanks. And sorry about all of this." After he left, she turned her attention to Shane. "You really should not have called the cops."

"Why?" Shane asked. "You do believe Raven, right?"

"I don't know, Shane. You heard the officer. This doesn't happen."

"This whole thing is bizarre and crazy, but one thing I know, Raven's not. I'm going to check on Ra-Ra," she said, leaving Marisa, Trent, Ashton, and Mrs. Haywood on the lawn. "And I'm going to get to the bottom of this," she screamed over her shoulder.

CHAPTER 23

Marisa

Mrs. Haywood looked so stressed out. She started to follow Shane into the house.

"Hold up a bit. I think she and Raven need some time together," Marisa said.

"Yeah," Mrs. Haywood said, wiping a tear from her eyes. "I'll go get dinner started." She looked like she had aged ten years. Brandi had gotten her looks from her mom, and her mom had aged well. But Brandi's disappearance was wearing on her.

"Okay, I'll be inside in a sec," Marisa told her. Then she turned to Trent and Ashton, who looked like they were a little bit stunned. "Thank you for bringing us over here. Guess you didn't expect all of this when we started talking. I understand if this is too much, Trent. I really do."

"Yo, Ashton, give me a minute to holler at Marisa please," he said to his best friend.

"No problem. Marisa, sorry about all of this," he said, getting into the car.

When they were alone, Trent looked down at Marisa. "You're right. I didn't know this would get so intense." He paused. "Or that I would come to respect you so much so quickly. You are awesome, Mari. You are strong, beautiful, and smart. I hate that you are going through this, but I am happy I can be here for you. Please don't ever think that it's too much for me."

How could I make it through this without him? Marisa thought. "Thanks, Trent," she said.

He reached out and hugged her. "Now get inside. Call me if you need anything," he said, giving her a small kiss on the cheek.

"I will," she nodded and turned to go inside the Haywood home. She headed straight to Brandi's room. Raven was sitting on Shane's lap.

"I knew nobody would believe me. I just knew it," Raven said.

"Ra-Ra, I told you ... it's not that I don't believe you. These are just questions that I have to ask you," Shane said.

"What's up?" Marisa asked.

"It was Brandi," Raven said, looking at Marisa square in the eyes.

Marisa sighed. "Okay, let's assume that it was Brandi."

"It was," Raven said, rolling her eyes.

"And let's assume that Raven has been hearing this same car pass by the house every day. Where do we go from there?" she questioned.

"Y'all could spend the night and help me look for this stupid car," Raven suggested.

"Now there's a plan," Shane said. "We look for the car ourselves."

"Okay, so we see the car. What are we going to do once we see it?" Marisa probed.

"I have an idea, but we need more hands on deck. We also need a couple of cars."

"What are you thinking?" Marisa asked her.

"What time do you normally hear the car pass?" Shane asked Raven.

"I'm usually in my room, my homework is done, and I'm watching TV, so six thirty, seven. Somewhere around then," Raven said, sounding older than her years.

"Well, it's six fifteen now," Marisa announced, sounding a bit nervous.

"No time like the present," Shane said. "Tonight, let's just see what happens."

"Then what?" Raven asked. "I've been peeping out the window for weeks. How does that get us closer to Brandi?"

"We have to follow that car. We have to see where it's going."

"That's crazy, Shane," Marisa paused and let out a deep sigh. "But you are right. If the person driving that car knows anything about what happened to Brandi, then we have to know who it is."

"It's six thirty," Raven announced. Her heart was pounding.

They were careful not to be seen as they peered through the window. Fifteen minutes passed. There was no sign of the black car. "Are you sure about the time?" Marisa asked her gently.

"Yeah, I'm sure," Raven said. She soon heard the familiar sound of the engine as it entered their street. "That's it!" she yelled. Just as Raven said, he gunned his engine when he was in front of the house and sped away.

"What in the world?" Shane asked, confused.

"Weird. Why does he do that? Why gun the engine that way?" Marisa asked.

"I don't know, but what I do know is that the car is a black Charger, and that driver is a fool. It's like he's taunting us."

"I told you," Raven said. "It's been happening since Brandi left, and I know it was the same car from that night."

"We should call the police," Marisa announced.

"They just left," Shane said, rolling her eyes. "They didn't believe us before, and they are not going to believe us a couple of hours later. No, I have a better idea."

Shane laid out her plan for the girls. Then she called Robin, and Marisa called Trent. They explained what was going to happen tomorrow after school.

"One way or another, we are going to find out if this guy knows anything about Brandi," Shane declared.

CHAPTER 24

Going In

The next evening everyone was in place. It was six thirty. Raven was in her room on the lookout for the black car. Shane, Marisa, and Robin were in Robin's car. Trent and Ashton were parked at the vacant house on the corner, ready to back out at any time. They were all on the phone together.

"Are you sure that he comes this way every day?" Robin asked anxiously. "We should have called the cops. This is so—"

Raven cut her off. "I hear the car!" she screamed into the phone.

"Oh my God," Marisa said. "Trent, Ashton, are you there?"

"Yeah, we're here."

"Okay, we are going to go right behind him. As soon as you start following us, we will turn off. Then it's all up to you to stay on his tail. Just stick to the plan. No matter where he takes you, follow him. Stay on the line so we can back you up if we need to." Shane had thought this through. *This has to work*, she thought.

The black Charger pulled up in front of the house and gunned the engine as it passed. "Idiot," Marisa whispered.

"We are on him. Pick up where we leave off. One of us has to stay on his tail. If he tries to leave the neighborhood, then you pick up at the four-way stop sign," Shane told Trent.

"Got it. We are pulling out behind you right now."

"Good. We are going to keep straight at the corner. Just stay on him," Shane said.

The situation was intense. Trent continued down the street undetected. They followed closely behind the black Charger but not for long. To their surprise, the Charger pulled into the driveway of a house only a few streets over.

"Um ... this can't be your guy," Trent announced, disappointed. "I've seen this dude before, but I can't remember where, and the house is too close for him to pull off a caper in his own neighborhood. No way. I don't see it."

"Where are you?" Marisa asked impatiently.

"The address is thirty-two fourteen Enclave. We are parked in the next block," Ashton told them.

"I'm turning that way now," Robin informed them.

"Okay, it's coming up now," Marisa said.

"*This* house?" Shane asked in disbelief.

"What?" Ashton asked. "You know this house?

"Yeah, this is where Brandi's friend grew up. This can't be a coincidence."

"Casey," Marisa said. "Her name was Casey Kennerson."

"Where are you? I'm coming over there," Raven told them.

"No, Ra-Ra, you stay at home where it's safe," Marisa told to her. "I promise we'll come by later. You did good, baby girl. Now hang up your phone."

"Let's hang up, guys, and meet at the park. We have to readjust the plan."

At the park, Robin pulled up next to Trent's car. "This is crazy," he announced, walking straight to Marisa. "So what's the story on Casey?"

"All I can remember," Marisa said, "is that Casey and Brandi were very close. It was right before she met us. There was some accident at a neighbor's swimming pool and she drowned."

"No, it was at the lake," Shane quietly corrected her.

"Well, who's the dude?" Ashton asked.

"I don't know," Marisa said.

"Me neither," Shane answered, "but we are about to find out."

Marisa and Shane implemented their new plan the next afternoon. Robin was to drive them to the Kennerson house and wait a couple of doors down. In another car, Trent and Ashton would keep an eye on the front door. At five thirty they were all in position.

"We are too late," Marisa said. "What if he comes home? Raven said that he sometimes swings by at six."

"Girl, we are in and out. Get the information as quickly as possible," Shane retorted. "Plus I gotta get outta this monkey suit as soon as possible."

"Oh, you make a cute cheerleader. Stop complaining."

They were both wearing Brandi's cheerleading outfits. They had gone to the store and purchased candy for a make-shift fundraiser for the PCH Cheerleading Squad.

When they rang the doorbell, a kind-faced woman opened the door. Her warm smile caught them by surprise. She was not what they expected. "Yes, how can I help you?" she asked.

"Yes, ma'am. The Port City High cheer-leaders are raising money for camp. Would you be interested in purchasing choco-late?" Shane flashed her killer smile.

"Oh, my husband is a dentist, but I have a weakness for chocolate. I'll help you out."

"That means so much to us," Marisa said innocently.

"Ma'am, I'm so sorry to ask, but it's an emergency. May I use your bathroom?" Shane asked sweetly.

"Of course. Come in, girls. My name is Mrs. Kennerson. You don't have to call me ma'am. Makes me feel so old," Mrs. Kennerson replied.

"Thanks so much, Mrs. Kennerson," Shane responded.

"It's down the hall, first door on the right," she told Shane.

But Shane wasn't interested in the bathroom. She snooped for clues. Located past the bathroom were two bedrooms: pink and blue. She went into the blue room and began her search.

Back in the front of the house, Marisa looked at a living room full of dated photos of two children: a boy and a girl. Nothing looked recent.

"Those are my babies when they were young," Mrs. Kennerson informed her.

"Oh, how old are they now?" Marisa asked.

Mrs. Kennerson lowered her head. "Well, Casey would have been your age, I think. She died when she was eight."

"I'm so sorry," Marisa said.

"Yes, it was hard on us, especially Steven. Losing Casey was definitely the hardest thing I have been through in my life. I felt like I lost Steven that day too," she said. "Oh, my, I've said too much. You probably didn't want to hear all of that."

"Oh no, ma'am, it's okay. I understand. That must have been hard," she said, wondering what was taking Shane so long.

"Well, I better check on your friend, make sure she's okay."

Marisa followed, talking loudly.

Shane had found something in a drawer. It looked like Brandi's locket. She was almost sure of it. She stuffed it in her pocket.

"What are you doing in here?" Mrs. Kennerson asked her in a stern voice.

"I ... I'm sorry Mrs. Kennerson. I was just admiring your home. Please forgive me," Shane said.

"You look as though you're doing more than admiring," she said, scolding Shane. She stopped as they all heard the front door open.

"Mom, where are you?" It was Steven. The first person he saw was Marisa. "What's going on here?" he asked as he approached his bedroom door. He looked panicked. As soon as he made eye contact with Shane, he bolted.

"Steven? Steven! What's going on?" Mrs. Kennerson shouted.

Marisa and Shane were right behind him. Shane screamed into her cell phone, "He's coming. Don't let him out of your sight! He had Brandi's locket."

"Explain yourself, young lady," Mrs. Kennerson shrieked, grabbing Marisa's arm. "What do you want with my son? What locket?"

"Steven has Brandi. We have to follow him!" Marisa yelled.

"Brandi Haywood? Casey's friend ..."

Mrs. Kennerson gasped in disbelief. "No! You're wrong."

"No, Mrs. Kennerson. We're right, it's him," Shane said calmly.

"I'm so ... Oh no ..." she said, collapsing into a chair close to the front door.

The girls ran to Robin's car and jumped in. "Go, go! We have to catch up to Trent and Ashton before they lose him."

CHAPTER 25

Brandi

Trent and Ashton were hot on Steven's trail. They could see him in his car, banging on the steering wheel.

Steven turned down a dirt road near the lake and abruptly stopped at a small house. He didn't notice that he was being followed. All he could think of was moving Brandi. He had to sedate her. So he went to the kitchen and slipped some Rohypnol into her water.

"Drink this," he ordered when he unlocked her door.

"No way! What's going on? Steven, you aren't drugging me again," she said coolly. She could see the fear in his eyes. She wanted to slow him down.

"You aren't safe here. Come with me, Casey," he ordered.

"Why did you call me that?" Brandi asked. She had been so stupid. She couldn't believe that she hadn't recognized him immediately. "Oh my God, Steven Kennerson," she gasped.

"We have to go," he said sternly.

"How could you?"

"How could I keep you safe, put you somewhere nice, and take care of you? Your family hasn't been there for you. Your dad cares more about drugs than you. Marisa and Shane are supposed to be your best friends and look what Marisa did to you with Matthew. Shane took her side. And then there's that loser, Brendon, who left you on the side of the road."

"How do you know all of that? I didn't tell you about it when we were online."

"I was always there for you, Brandi," he said, trying to hold her hand, but she pulled away. "When I came home, I saw you at Jerry's with Brendon. I saw your face when you saw Matthew and Marisa together."

"How? Where *were* you?" And then she remembered. "You work there! You've watched my every move. You stole my purse? My keys? That's how you were able to take my things. *It was all you.*"

"I needed those things to be able to help you. Don't you see that? Now you have to drink this. I promise I'll never let them hurt you again."

"No! I won't go with you."

"You don't have a choice. Now drink it! There's no time for games."

"Why isn't there time? What's happened?" And then it dawned on her. "They know. They are on to you."

"Nobody believes your silly little friends. They've called the police before, and nothing happened. They're not coming."

"So why the rush, huh?"

Suddenly, there was a pounding on the door. This was something that Brandi had not heard since she'd been here. "I'm in here!" she tried to scream, but Steven clamped his hand over her mouth.

Steven panicked. He squeezed her jaws open, pouring the liquid into her mouth. Brandi could feel herself begin to choke. She had no choice but to drink. She felt herself slipping away.

Steven threw Brandi over his shoulder and headed out the back toward the lake.

The scene was all too familiar to Steven. It was just like the day Casey died. She'd ridden on his back down to the water. They were going to take Dad's rowboat out. It was a beautiful spring day.

Contrary to what their parents always told them, they had gone on the water without their life jackets. Everything had happened so fast. Casey stood up to adjust the rickety old seat she was sitting on, then they hit something. And she went flying into the water.

She was a good swimmer, so Steven thought she would pop right back up. But she didn't. "Casey!" he screamed as he dove into the murky lake. But he couldn't find her. By the time he located his sister, it was too late.

Steven was never the same. The Kennersons tried everything to reach their son, but nothing worked. They finally had him admitted to a mental health facility, hoping for professional help.

As he ran out to the water with Brandi across his shoulder, Steven remembered Casey and sobbed. "I'll always keep you safe," he whispered to Brandi. "Always."

CHAPTER 26

Marisa

I see them!" Marisa screamed as her long legs ran as fast as she could to catch the man carrying her best friend. "Brandi, Brandi!" she yelled after them. But Steven didn't slow or look back as he ran wildly toward the water.

Marisa was the only one who saw Steven. Everyone else was still at the front of the lake house trying to get in. Trent, Ashton, Robin, and Shane never heard Marisa's cry for help or her screaming Brandi's name. She was on her own.

Marisa chased Steven to the water's

edge. He looked confused. His eyes were wild and empty. "Steven," she tried to talk calmly, "you have to put Brandi down. You have to let her go now."

"You don't care about her. You just care about yourself. She told me about you and Matthew and how you hurt her. You were never her friend," he spat.

"That's not true. Brandi was ready to move on. Too bad she moved on to you pretending to be someone you weren't. You are the one who hurt her," she said defensively.

"That's not what she says, Marisa."

"Well, you let me ask her that myself." She walked toward him, but that made him move closer to the water. "Let her go!" Marisa yelled, growing increasingly upset.

"I'll never let her go. She's not going back to that miserable life. She's coming with me."

"B! You have to wake up," she urged, turning her attention to Brandi. But Brandi didn't move. "What did you do to her? You let her go now!" Without thinking, she picked up a thick branch and lunged for Steven, forcing him to drop Brandi.

She had a brief moment to swing at Steven and she connected. He fell to the ground, and she stood over Brandi, trying to wake her up.

"B! Please," she said, shaking a groggy Brandi, who was not responding. "Pl—" she tried to say again but was slapped by an angry Steven, who had quickly recovered.

Marisa crumpled to the ground next to Brandi. Steven seemed confused as to what to do next. The boat that used to be tied to the dock was no longer there. He could see another boat tied to a neighboring dock. They had to make their way across the lake if they were going to get away. He scooped Brandi into his arms and ran.

CHAPTER 27

Shane

"Where is Mari?" Shane asked Trent as they both reached the back of the house. "I thought she was with you."

"No, Ashton was with me trying to find a window or something that would get us inside."

"Marisa!" Shane screamed. She could feel it in her bones. Something was wrong. "Marisa!"

"I'm going down to the lake!" Trent shouted anxiously.

Ashton was close behind him. "Dude, this is crazy!"

They could see Marisa lying on the ground. Blood poured from a gash on her face. "Oh no," Trent said. "Go, go!" he yelled at Ashton, who quickly surveyed the scene. He could see someone running in the distance. Shane caught his gaze, and they ran as hard as they could to catch up to Steven, who had just arrived at the boat and was trying to get it untied.

"No!" Shane screamed. "Hurry, Ashton! We have to stop him!" It wasn't looking good. There was no way that they would be able to reach him before he had the boat in the water. In the other direction, a pregnant Robin ran slowly trying to catch up to Steven too. To Shane's surprise, Mrs. Kennerson was close behind Robin.

When she spotted her son, she yelled his name. Her voice seemed to stop him in his tracks. His head popped up from the task at hand. He looked confused. "Baby, don't do this," Mrs. Kennerson yelled. "Let Brandi go!"

"I'm sorry, Mom. I can't do that! I have to take care of her!" he yelled.

"Son, she's not Casey," Mrs. Kennerson said, walking closer to her son, smiling at him softly. "And no matter what you do, it won't bring Casey back. Now you have to make this right."

"Mama, this *is* right. I'm going to take care of Brandi. You'll see. I'll keep her safe."

Mrs. Kennerson could feel her son's pain. "I'm sorry, baby. I miss her too, but Casey wouldn't have wanted this for Brandi. You have to let her go."

"But, Mama ... "

"No, baby. You are going to let her go. The police are on their way, and so is Brandi's family. I called them. When the girls told me that you might have Brandi, I knew there was only one place you would take her. It was the last place you and Casey were together."

"I didn't mean to hurt her. I just wanted to help." He began to sob.

"Come on, son. Let's get you some help." By this time, Mrs. Kennerson had slowly made her way to the boat. She took her son's hand and led him away from Brandi. Ashton ran to the boat and scooped her up, carrying her still limp body to the grass.

"Brandi," Shane pleaded, checking her pulse. "You have to wake up, honey." They could hear the sirens in the background. The cops were getting closer. Trent held a shaken Marisa, who was determined to be by her best friend's side when she opened her eyes. Robin held Brandi's hand tightly.

Finally, they could see a flutter of movement in her eyes. "She's in there," Marisa said. The drugs were slowly wearing off, but Brandi didn't know where she was. It had been a long two months in captivity. It seemed like years ago that she had been taken from her friends and family. She wasn't sure if she was dreaming or not. Whatever it was, it felt good.

Just as Brandi's eyes began to open fully, Raven came running across the grass. When Mrs. Kennerson called the Haywood home, Brandi's mother began to scream in relief. Raven watched as her mother fell to the ground like a ragdoll. She kept saying, "She's alive. My baby is alive." They loaded up in the car and followed the directions that Mrs. Kennerson had given her.

Raven was out of the car before either of her parents. She was determined to get to her sister as quickly as possible. She threw her body on the ground next to Brandi, whose head rested on Shane's lap. "I knew you were alive. I knew it," Raven whispered. Shane hugged them both as Raven held tightly to her sister.

"Hey, baby girl," was all that Brandi could manage to say. As Brandi looked at their faces for the first time in months, she knew that this had been just as hard on them as it had been on her.

Brandi's mom and dad ran alongside the gurney as the paramedics crossed the grass to treat Brandi and Marisa. Someone called the reporters. There were cameras everywhere capturing the spectacular rescue. Finally, Brandi Haywood was going home.

TAKEN

Epilogue

When the police arrived at the scene, they searched everywhere for Steven, but he was not to be found. They went to the Kennerson's home, to his father's office, but nobody had seen him. Even Mrs. Kennerson had disappeared. When she showed up a week later, she was questioned about his whereabouts. She told them Steven was getting the help he needed. He wouldn't bother anyone again. She didn't budge when the police threatened to jail her. If he was in a mental health facility like his mother insisted, it wasn't in Texas.

There was no comfort in his relocation for Brandi. Somewhere in the back of her mind, he was still out there.

Brandi didn't return to school that spring, but she knew that she couldn't miss the school play. Marisa and Shane had worked so hard, and she couldn't let them down. As she prepared to go out in public for the first time since her abduction, there was a knock on her bedroom door.

"Yes?" she said. It was her father. It looked as though he had taken her disappearance harder than anyone else.

"Hey, honey. You have a minute?"

"Yeah, I'm just getting ready for the play. The curtain's going up soon."

"You just make sure that you stay close to Mom and keep Raven close too. You still have to be careful. That guy's still out there—"

"Dad," she cut him off, "I refuse to live my life scared. I'm not afraid of Steven."

"Yeah, I know. You are a very brave girl. That's kind of what I wanted to talk to you about." He paused. "Daddy's about to go away for a while."

Brandi kept combing her hair. "Okay, same place again?" she asked.

"No, it's a different rehab ... in San Antonio. It's supposed to be really good. I'm going to get better this time, Brandi. I feel like I'm the reason that all of this happened to you."

She walked over to her bed where he sat. "Dad, how could you have been the reason?" she asked.

"I haven't been there for you and Raven. I've been so caught up in my own issues that you girls have gone without a man in your lives. Not anymore. It ends here."

Opening night for *The Wizard of Oz* was packed. Luckily Brandi, Raven, and her mom had tickets for front row seats. Everyone was so happy to see Brandi. She could tell that they didn't know what to say, but she understood. When the cheerleaders spotted her, they swarmed her, hugging her and almost knocking her to the ground. Even Christina had not been invited to the house since Brandi's return. She hugged Brandi tightly and cried. "Don't ever leave again," she warned her.

"I wouldn't dream of it," Brandi said, smiling at her friend.

"Come on, baby. The play is about to start," Mrs. Haywood said to her.

"Gotta go. Still roommates for camp, right?" she asked Christina.

"Definitely. Who else could put up with me?"

"Okay, we'll get together about decorations for our room. See you soon." Brandi could feel herself piecing her life back together. *Thank you, God, for bringing me home.*

The cast got a standing ovation. Shane and Marisa's performance was stellar. It was a magical night. They met up in the foyer when they were done. Brandi's mother was taking them out for a celebratory meal. The abduction had changed her too. Brandi finally felt like she had her mother's support.

"Jerry's?" Brandi asked as they got in her mom's Acura.

"You don't want to take a break from Jerry's?" Marisa asked, worried.

"Yeah, let's go somewhere else," Shane said.

"We have been going to Jerry's since seventh grade. It's a tradition I'm not going to break. I'm okay, y'all," she insisted. "Now let's go eat some burgers."

"Sounds good to me," Raven said with enthusiasm. "I'm going to need some ice cream, though. Where's Trent?" Everyone laughed.

Jerry's was packed, judging by the full parking lot. "We'll never find a seat in this crowd. I guess this wasn't a good idea after all. And I'm starving," Brandi said.

"I think we'll be okay," Mrs. Haywood said to her daughter as they exited the car.

When Brandi walked in, she heard a loud "Surprise!" She looked around. All of her friends were there. Her hands covered her mouth and tears ran down her face.

Trent and Ashton both picked her up in huge bear hugs. Her ex-boyfriend, Matthew, was there full of smiles. The cheerleaders and their sponsor were there. Everybody who meant anything to Brandi was in Jerry's. Even the owner shook her hand. Then standing in front of her table with a dozen white roses was her father. She looked at the handsome man in front of her, and she felt like a little girl again.

Raven ran to be by her sister's side. "I'm so happy you're home, Brandi."

"Thanks to you, Raven. Thank you for never giving up on me." She gave her sister a huge hug. "Okay, no more tears, everybody! Let's eat!" she announced happily, enjoying every minute of her welcome home party.

ABOUT THE AUTHOR

Shannon Freeman

$\mathcal{B}$orn and raised in Port Arthur, Texas, Shannon Freeman works full time as an English teacher in her hometown. After completing college at Oral Roberts University, Freeman began her work in the classroom teaching English and oral communications. At that time, the characters of her breakout series, Port City High, began to form, but these characters would not come to life for years. An apartment fire destroyed almost all of the young teacher's worldly possessions before she could begin writing. With nothing to lose, Freeman packed up and headed to Los Angeles, California, to pursue a passion that burned within her since her youth, the entertainment industry.

Beginning in 2001, Freeman made numerous television appearances and enjoyed a rich life full of friends and hard work. In 2008, her world once again changed when she and her husband, Derrick Freeman, found out that they were expecting their first child. Freeman then made the difficult decision to return to Port Arthur and start the family that she had always wanted.

At that time, Freeman returned to the classroom, but entertaining others was still a desire that could not be quenched. Being in the classroom again inspired her to tell the story of Marisa, Shane, and

Brandi that had been evolving for almost a decade. She began to write and the Port City High series was born.

Port City High is the culmination of Freeman's life experiences, including her travels across the United States and Europe. Her stories reflect the friendships she's made across the globe. Port City High is the next breakout series for today's young adult readers. Freeman says, "The topics are relevant and life changing. I just hope that people are touched by my characters' stories as much as I am."